Ruby

Mail Order Brides of Witchita Falls

RUBY: MAIL ORDER BRIDES OF WITCHITA FALLS

by

Cyndi Raye

To a brand new beginning.

Mail Order Brides of Witchita Falls

Cyndi Raye

Table of Contents

Chapter 1

"Mama," Ruby whispered.

Her mother's fragile hand reached out, stroking Ruby's cheeks. She tried to speak, struggling to get the words out. "It's urgent you leave here, today," she gasped.

Ruby shook her head back and forth, scared for the first time in her life. She knew her mama was going to die, the sickness had been going on for some time now. Today was so real she could barely contain her fear. She leaned her face into the soft, warm hand. "I can't leave you like this."

"You must. I have something for you." Ruby felt the instant loss when her mama's hand left her face. She wanted to curl up along side of her and hold on to her so tight in hopes the only person who ever loved her would not leave yet. How cruel of God to do this to her now! How could He take her away and leave Ruby to face life alone? She wanted to stand up and shake a fist in the air, but it wouldn't be proper to do so in front of her mother, whose staunch faith had kept her alive far longer than the doctor predicted.

A bout of coughing stirred Ruby from her awful thoughts. She grabbed a clean linen from the night stand and dabbed it across her mama's mouth as a tiny pool of blood trickled from the corner. Her mother struggled to sit up in bed. Ruby cast a worried glance to Tillo, who had taken care of the two of them from the time they came to live at her uncle's brownstone manor in New York City when Ruby was a small baby.

The older woman frowned before shaking her head sadly and helped to pull the dying woman up against the pillows. She tucked the blanket under her mama's chin, muttering words so soft Ruby couldn't make them out.

"I'm fine," mama said, raising her beautiful blue eyes to her daughter. Ruby watched as life came back in to them and smiled. Her mother was so brave and strong. She had proven it so many times over the years. She opened her mouth to take a sip of the laudanum Tillo offered, then pulled back with a slight shake of her head. A frail hand pushed the bottle away. "Later, Till. I need to give my Ruby something. Hand me my bible."

Tillo picked up the worn book and laid it on her lap. Ruby watched with saddened and yet curious eyes as her mother opened the leather bound book. Long, slender fingers ran over the edge of the folded papers inside the pages. She looked up at Ruby and smiled. "This is your ticket out, child. Come here." Her other hand patted the quilt as Ruby sat down on the edge of the bed.

"What do you mean, my ticket out, Mama?"

"Your uncle thinks I owe him for living here all these years, even though I've paid my way all along, thanks to these. I've cashed in my share of land certificates to save his struggling business every single time he needed help. His were gone the first year our lawyers gave them to us." Her chest rose and fell before another coughing fit started. Ruby was used to seeing her like this and hated how much pain her mama was in.

"Maybe you should drink the laudanum, Mama."

A hand touched her own. "Not yet. I rescued him many times but he's in trouble again. These last certificates I've saved for you. I told him there are no more. Do not let him find these."

Ruby glanced at the papers being handed to her. The edges shook as her mama tried to shove them in her hand. "What am I supposed to do with these?"

Her mother leaned back against the pillows and smiled as if a wonderful memory passed over her. She sighed as the papers hit the quilt. "You keep them for now. They are worth a fortune in the West. People are leaving the city in droves to find a new life where the air is pure and the city dust is far behind. You can sell these for cash or buy your own land. I was there once."

"You were?" Ruby leaned closer. She had heard this story many times before and never tired of listening to her tales. "Tell me, Mama."

"I met your father out West. I traveled the new rail road to visit Aunt Adeline, who was the first family member to use her land certificates. She purchased a piece of land along the rail road line, build a boarding house and made quite the life for herself."

Ruby remembered the stories of her Aunt Adeline. A smile slipped across her face at the intensity of the way the woman paved a way for herself. She wanted to meet her so bad, but they never got the chance to travel as promised since mama got sick a few years back.

Her mother's voice was becoming weak but Ruby didn't have the heart to stop her. "Wesley worked for the rail road. We fell in love and I was completely smitten. We got married and planned on using my land certificates to build a ranch and farm the land. I remember a trickling waterfall, where he proposed to me one Saturday afternoon. He said we would buy the land surrounding the flowing water. He was ready to settle down, away from the rail road." Her voice cracked as tears spilled down her cheeks.

"Mama, please. Don't wear yourself out."

Tillo picked up the bottle of opium for another try. "Come on, Misses, please take some medicine."

Her mama, sweat pouring from her brow, finally nodded, allowing Tillo to tilt the rim of the bottle to her mouth. Ruby watched as her head fell back against the feather pillows, silent as the pain began to fade away. Her mother's eyes began to droop, her breathing even now. "Finish the story, Till," she whispered, saving her strength.

Ruby's heart pounded inside. With eyes like her mothers, she raised them to the roof of the bedroom, silently berating God for giving her mother this affliction. She wanted to cry out, now more than ever and shame the very one whom her mother had trusted all these years.

A calloused hand covered her own. She looked into Tillo's troubled dark eyes. "It won't do any good to curse the man upstairs."

"I hate that God did this to her."

Tillo patted her hand. "Oh child, ain't no God who did this, it just happened."

When the door burst open, Ruby was glad her mother was drugged. She could hear Uncle Ross's short bursts of breaths as he carted his overweight body in to the room, uninvited of course. "The sickness is her retribution for defying our parents years ago. Running off to that uncivilized, savage territory out west against their wishes comes with punishment. I knew it would come back to haunt her. I told her so, over and over." He pointed a finger at Ruby. "Now you will have to pay for her punitive measures."

Ruby wanted to spit in his eye but refrained. She bit her lip when Tillo grabbed her hand and squeezed to keep her calm. It also helped to keep her in her seat when Uncle Ross leaned his fat body over her mother and pressed an ear close to her nose, as if he wanted to see if she were still breathing.

"I'm. Not dead. yet."

Ross jumped as if the very devil himself came out of her mama. It almost made Ruby laugh at the way his body fat jiggled when he jumped back. She also didn't miss the fact Tillo shoved the land certificates under her mama's quilt before Ross noticed them.

Uncle Ross glared at Ruby. "Mark my words, Ruby. You will find out your fate the moment my sister takes her last breath."

"You have no right to come in here like this," she told him, placing a hand on her hip. He had been overbearing and rude since she was a child and she hated him for being so mean. Even if he did give them a home, it came at a price. She wanted to lash out, tell him it was his fault too that her mama was dying but refrained from doing so.

He shrugged as dark, hateful eyes bore into her own. Ruby was shaking from the top of her head to the tips of of her toes for defying the man who gave them a home years ago but it couldn't be helped. She refused to let him ruin the time her mother had left. He took a step towards her, his finger pointing. "Just as I suspected, you're origins are showing with that smart mouth. No lady would behave in such a discerning manner."

Uncle Ross took her wrist in the palm of his hand and squeezed. "Ouch," she muttered. "Let me alone." It was offensive the way he leaned in to speak. Fear struck at her heart. He had never crossed the line with her when her mother was healthy. She had always kept him in place. Would he hurt her? What was to become of her when mama was gone?

He leaned in and whispered for her ears alone. "I have plans for you. Big plans. Just ask Horace Lourdes. He has had his eye on you for a long, long time. You're just what I need to pay off my debt." He whipped his hand away when Ruby's mama called out.

"Leave. Ross. Don't force me to tell your secrets. Ruby. Come here." It didn't take long for the man to leave, banging the door shut. Ruby grabbed her wrist, rubbing it with her other hand. She clamoured to her mother's side.

"Why is he so mean, Mama, and what does he mean that I'm just what he needs?"

"My worst fear has come true." She struggled with her words, the opiums affect making it difficult for her to talk. "You must leave, child. Today."

Ruby shook her head back and forth. "I'm not leaving you like this, Mama. Never."

"Till, explain to her what will happen." Her eyes fluttered shut. Tillo began to dab a cloth into the water basin, wringing it out and placing it over her forehead.

"Sit down, Ruby," the woman ordered.

Ruby did as she was told. Something was off. There was more to this story than she knew. Perhaps it was time she listened. "Tell me everything, Tillo. I want to know."

Tillo nodded as she continued to bath her misses. "When your father got killed, your mama knew there was no way she could make it out west. She came back here with a babe in her arms. She begged her parents to forgive her for running away but they banned her from ever stepping foot in their presence again. The only one who took her in was your uncle. At a price, I might add. At the time all she wanted to do was put a roof over your head. You were a wee thing without any means to survive." Tillo's voice lowered as she continued the story, "The thing is, your uncle has a gambling problem. His wife left him because he owed bad men. She couldn't take it any longer and fled to her home in the South, never to be seen again. At least that's the story the man has told. I think there's more to it and your mama knows what happened but she's been loyal to her brother. Not sure why, he is a bad man."

Tillo wrung out the cloth again, placing it on her mama's forehead. The steady rhythm of her breathing kept Ruby calm. She didn't know where this story was going. "Now, child, none of this is your fault, you hear me?"

At her nod, Tillo continued, "Your mama was desperate, like I said, she needed to raise you up. Your uncle bargained with her for you. He said when you are at the age of marriage, you must marry Horace Lourdes, his long-time friend, the one he is indebted to. I remember that day, the two of you standing on the doorstep, having no choice but to agree to his terms."

Ruby's eyes widened. "I, I don't believe mama would bargain like that. She wouldn't give me up to a man that could be my grandfather!"

A wince came from her mama. "I lied. Never planned to do it, I swear."

"Now, now, misses. You rest, let me do the explaining."

"No." The strong voice coming from the bed shocked Ruby. Her mother was so weak and yet the voice was so bold. As if she had more energy in that moment, the frail woman pulled herself up in bed until she was sitting straight up. "It's my story and I want Ruby to know everything. I did bargain for you, Ruby, and I'm sorry. I didn't know what else to do, where else to turn. My parents banned me, the streets weren't safe for a baby and I couldn't let us be homeless. You may wonder why I didn't sell the land certificates. It's because the money would eventually run out. I couldn't take the chance. Living here with Ross was the only way to raise you right. I was young. I kept those certificates, believing some day we would go back. I never planned to keep my promise to him. Now, I'm dying, plain and simple. It's too late for me, but not for you. Here." She took the notes in her hand and handed them to Ruby.

"Where did these come from, Mama?"

"I'm feeling light as a feather right now, so I best get it all out before I can't go on. An ancestor of ours was a gambler, like your uncle, 'cept he was good at it. He won these land certificates in a poker game. They are like gold. You can buy land with these, whatever land you want, where ever you go, if no one has claimed the land, it's yours by way of these certificates. Now that Wichita Falls is becoming modernized, I thought we could go back, buy a small place and live there, the two of us. But my plans went awry when I got consumption. It may be too late for me, but not for you. Get on that train as fast as you can and claim your land. Tillo has your ticket. I instructed her to buy it a few days ago. Do it before Ross makes you marry Lourdes."

Ruby sat so still she wasn't sure she dare move. Not only was the person who loved her more than life itself leaving her, she was inclined to leave everything she ever knew to start over. In the West. With cowboys and Indians and outlaws. She had read the penny novels, romanticized at times about meeting a cowboy and living happily ever after like she read in those tall tales. She just never dreamed she would be heading into the midst of it.

"Ruby? I'm sorry."

"Mama. I'll do my best. I'll make you proud." She swore in that moment she would never let a man like her uncle tell her what to do. No, she would follow her mother's dream and head westward, defining a life for herself no one could take away. She remembered the stories about her brave Aunt Adeline, who forged a life on the frontier. Yes, she smiled to herself. She would be like her, a brave and powerful woman of the west and nothing in this world would stop her.

Chapter 2

Except maybe a thief and scoundrel. "Get back here!" Ruby pulled up her skirts to chase the little rotten thief who stole her reticule right out of her hands. She had been waiting patiently at the train station, minding her own business when something brushed by her skirts. It had happened so quickly. Ruby had been opening the reticule in order to pull out her ticket when the little varment snatched the cloth bag. He ran down the boarded walk, the skinny body zig-zagging around people trying to board the train. Ruby took off after him, trying to catch up but it wasn't so easy with long skirts that got in the way. She placed booted heel after heel, trying to dodge around the passengers to no avail. At the end of the walk she stopped, pushing strands of hair back that fell from her bun.

Shielding her eyes with her hand, looking for him in the crowds, Ruby realized the implication of getting robbed. Fear took a hold of her in the recesses of her gut. Without a ticket to board the train, all would be lost. Then her face drained of color. The land certificates were in the reticule, too. "Oh no, no, no!" Defeat fell upon her shoulders as she made an attempt to leave the platform to follow the boy in to the streets. She stopped when realizing there was no use. The boy had gotten away. He had escaped to an area where it wasn't proper for a woman to be alone. Ruby was brave but not stupid. Someone like her didn't belong in those streets. She'd be ravished and left for dead. Was that how her mother had felt so long ago? A new understanding came upon her as she realized the agony of making a decision to ask someone like Uncle Ross for help, but when it came down to the cold, hard facts, her mama had no choice.

There had to be another way to get her ticket back. Determined, Ruby marched up to the conductor. "Pardon me, sir. Are you running this train?"

He tipped his hat and nodded. "Ma'am, what can I do for you?"

"My reticule was stolen by a young thief. I had my ticket in there and I'd like to claim another since that one won't be used by me."

The conductor chuckled. "I'm sorry, miss. We can't give you another ticket. When did you purchase the one you claim to have had?" he asked. The skeptical look wasn't lost on Ruby. He doubted she ever had one in the first place.

"I swear there was a ticket bought yesterday. My mama's maid came down here to purchase one. Wouldn't the rail road have proof?"

"I'm afraid I don't have time to help you. This train leaves in fifteen minutes. If what you say is true, go get your mama's maid to verify with the ticket holder and you can catch the next train out in a few days."

"A few days will be too late. I need to get to Wichita Falls," Ruby confessed. She bit her lip and looked around. There was no way she could go back to the Brownstone. Slipping away in the early morning was hard enough. When Uncle Ross finds out she left, he would be furious. It was bad enough he cornered her later that evening to threaten her again with marriage to the old coot he owed money to. He told her within a day of her mother's passing, he'd have her married off. Then he laughed and slapped her shoulder so hard she wanted to kick him. He was an abusive, horrible, selfish man.

When she had threatened to leave, he had locked her in her own room. Little did he realize she knew a way out. She had done it many times before, climbing out the window, working her way across the limb, then sliding down the trunk of the tree to meet some of her friends in her younger days. At eighteen, Ruby had a harder time of it, but when her feet hit the side walk, she took off down the street swearing never to return again.

There was no way she could go back.

A tear slipped from her cheek. Ruby lowered herself to a bench at the station, setting her one piece of luggage on the ground, her shoulders slumping with defeat. She never saw the couple holding hands beside her.

What was she going to do?

Where would she go?

Would she be inclined to go back to the Brownstone and

marry an old man? Ruby almost gagged thinking about marriage to Horace Lourdes.

"Here."

Eyes closed, head tipped towards the ground, Ruby slowly brought her gaze towards the female voice to see a gloved hand holding something. A train ticket dangled in front of her.

"Pardon?" Ruby asked, more confused than ever.

"I won't be needing this after all," the woman said. She snuggled closer to the man beside her.

"I thank you but I can't possibly take your ticket. I have no money to pay you. The boy, he robbed me, took everything I had."

"It's fine. I never paid for this either. Here." She reached in her own reticule and pulled out some letters wrapped with twine. "You better get on the train or it will leave without you. I heard you say you were going to Wichita Falls. This ticket will take you there."

"Are you sure?" At the woman's nod, Ruby reached out and took the ticket and letters before rushing towards the train. A whoosh of air brushed against her skirts and she turned back but didn't notice anything strange. There were a few stragglers like her trying to board last minute. Perhaps that was what brushed by her, another passenger trying to get aboard.

"Please tell him I'm sorry but I found my true love. He was here all along."

"What? Tell who?"

The lady who gave her the tickets laughed and waved as she

rose from the bench. "Read the letters," she shouted, cupping her hands around her mouth to shout out at Ruby.

Clutching them in her hand, Ruby worked her way to a seat in the middle of the rail car. She was glad it wasn't full. Sitting by the window, her gaze fell to the hustle and bustle of New York City and was glad to leave it all behind. Closing her eyes, she sighed, letting the sound of the train rattling down the track lull her to sleep. This new adventure was about to change her life.

Marshall Montgomery raised a booted heel to the fallen limb. With a quick kick, it moved out of his way so he could bring the wagon over to load it up. A treacherous storm passing through his land earlier fell some limbs and trees on the property. It would take hours to clean up the mess.

"Sorta looked like a large funnel just ploughed right through, huh, boss?"

He nodded to Max, the foreman of his ranch, glad to have the man along to help. The other men were checking the ranch land, making sure the rest of the cows and steers made it through the storm. There were 5 men in all, 6 including him. He was proud of his accomplishments so far. Before long, the ranch would be a big homestead, hiring more and more men each year. A dream come true. It sure beat working on the rail road. Those days were over now that he had his own spread.

Thanks to the land certificates he bought while working as a surveyor for the rail road. He had hesitated at first, thinking he'd always stay with the rail road but as they traveled further west, connecting towns, the land began to draw him in. He had ached to begin a new life and when the rail road tracks were laid in Wichita Falls and he saw the beauty of the area, Marshall threw down his tools and turned in the certificates for land. Six hundred forty acres of raw land was all his.

Marshall's next goal was to buy more of the area next to his but he needed one more cattle drive to do so. It was a shame he had to spend some of his savings on a train ticket but it couldn't be helped. Well, two train tickets. One for his little nephew from New York City, who lost his parents recently. The other, well, that had been a dumb move. Or maybe not. Maybe it was time he settled down.

"When's the boy getting here?" Max asked, bringing Marshall back to reality.

He shrugged. "In a few days. I'll meet him at the station in town."

"Ya probably want to wear your Sunday best for that trip, seeing ya also bought yourself a mail order bride."

"Yeah, and I may have had too much whiskey that day. I'm regretting it already but I can't go back on my word now. Besides, the boy needs a woman to replace my sister. I don't know what to do with a little person."

Max snickered. "Seems you'll find out right soon enough."

Marshall took off his hat and slid his hand through dark, thick hair. He gazed over the land, trying to see it as a stranger would. Even though he agreed to this mail order bride stuff, he wondered if a city woman would be happy here. It took a lot of gumption to love the wild frontier. Not too many ladies from the east dared to venture further than the Mississippi River.

When the rail road came to Wichita Falls, men began to settle here. But the ladies were few and far between. When Miss Adeline from the boarding house began to dabble in her new business of bringing mail order brides to town, it seemed to work. The rowdy town was beginning to settle somewhat. More families were filling the streets instead of drunken cowboys and rail road workers looking for a cheap thrill.

Before, there had been a rail road depot, a saloon and mercantile. Since Miss Adeline began her mail order business, the town was growing fast. They now had a church and parish, side streets with cabins and rows of houses along the main road with families and men looking to start a family. The Texas prairie was blooming with life.

He had been walking to his horse, well, stumbling to it one late afternoon drinking at the saloon, sad over his sisters death, when Miss Adeline confronted him. He hadn't seen her in over ten years, never even met the son she wrote so much about.

Miss Adeline had heard his sister died and knew he was bringing the boy out here. After a lecture on how the boy needed a firm hand and a mother to learn him, she had made Marshall feel so guilty he signed right up for her mail order bride. After that, he had exchanged letters with a lady from New York City. Catherine Jackson.

Now he would be meeting her within a few days. She mentioned she wanted a fresh start, somewhere far away from the lure of the city. She loved horses and would be an asset to his ranch. Said she didn't mind working hard and could take care of herself. Said she could cook and clean and was fit enough to do outside work if needed. With those credentials, he figured she'd be good for the boy and could replace Joe doing the cooking. He needed Joe out on the ranch more than in the cook house.

"Watch that limb, boss."

Max's warning brought his attention back to the business at hand. A snake slithered along the fallen limb, a rattler. Marshall stepped back, too close for comfort until he had enough space between them to strike it down with his axe. He looked up at his foreman. "Thanks."

Max nodded. "Best to keep your mind on the work at hand, boss. Don't mean no disrespect but we can't have you getting bitten here with you becoming a new father and husband soon."

Marshall glared at his foreman. "Guess you're right," he told Max after a bit. "It wouldn't do any good for the boy to come all this way to a dead uncle. Then the kid would have to go back to the city to grandparents who don't want him."

"What's the story with the boy? He's ten? Sounds like he's old enough to help with some of the ranch work," Max suggested.

Marshall shrugged, then swung the axe at the tree limb. "Got a letter from my brother-in-laws family. Said the boy was living with his grandparents after my sister and her husband died in the carriage accident. He won't listen, keeps running away, hanging out in the back alleys of the city, skipping school. As soon as I heard, I sent a one way ticket for him to come out here. I had just finished my business with mailing the letter, had a few drinks at the saloon. That's when I got reprimanded by Miss Adeline about how a boy needed a mother. You know how fast your business is spread all over town around here. Personally, I think Miss Adeline coerced me into taking a mail order bride."

Max flung his head back and laughed. "That's Addie. She's got half the town matched up with someone. Glad I'm not there much these days."

Marshall's brow rose. "That's cause she's sweet on you, Max. The last time we went to town together, I saw the way the two of you talked. I'd say it's the reason she hasn't found you a bride yet."

Max shook his head. "Not true. We're friends since way back."

"You may want to rethink things. Friend's don't blush like she does whenever you're around."

Max moved away without saying anything, ending the conversation. He began to work on another tree. Marshall didn't mean to embarrass him but the man was blind as a bat. Everyone could tell Miss Adeline was sweet on him. Everyone except the man himself. Or, maybe he was just good at hiding his feelings.

Marshall was glad he wasn't going to go sweet on a woman. He didn't have that kind of time. This mail order bride seemed nice enough. Catherine. Her name rolled of his tongue nicely but he didn't think she was looking for love. She wanted a way out of the city. She was a hard worker, could cook and clean and work outside in the garden. Guess a man couldn't ask for much more than that in a woman.

Chapter 3

Ruby woke to the sound of passengers moving towards the dining car. She was so hungry, actually ravished. With her uncle locking her away in the bedroom all night, there hadn't been a way for her to stock up on food for the trip. Now, with her reticule stolen, the extra money she tucked away was long gone. She would have to do without food until they reached Wichita Falls. It was going to be a long couple of days.

"Care to join us for supper?" a voice said behind her.

As she turned to see who was talking, Ruby smiled at the odd fellow. Wearing a top hat that looked way too big for his head, a giggle almost erupted. She contained herself by placing a hand over her mouth and coughing. "I'm afraid that's impossible," she told him. "My reticule has been stolen with all my monies inside."

The man lifted his hat and tipped it at her. "You have to be careful traveling alone these days. It's quite alright. I am inviting you to dine, therefore I plan to pay for your meal ticket."

Ruby hesitated. The man looked harmless. Dare she let him? Would a lady alone be scoured by allowing a stranger to feed her?

"Don't worry. My wife is right here. We'd be happy to escort you to the dining car."

Ruby looked behind the man to see a tiny figure. She hadn't noticed the woman until she peeked her head over his shoulder. That's when she realized the two were standing, not sitting. Her mouth hung open for a slight second before she chastised herself for staring. "I'm sorry. I didn't see her," Ruby apologized.

"Quite alright, miss. You are not the first to notice our size is not normal. We are tiny people. May I introduce you to Mrs. Martin."

The little woman stepped around her husband. She held a reticule over her wrist in one hand and held her other one out. Ruby took the tiny warm hand in her own. "Nice to meet you, Mrs. Martin. I am Ruby Adams of New York City."

"A pleasure, dear. I'm famished. How about you?" She began to walk towards the dining car.

"Yes. I believe I will take you up on your offer. Thank you." With relief, she followed the Mrs. to a table with a stunning view of the landscape. The dining attendant helped the two tiny people on to their chairs as if they were royalty, then held the chair for her.

Ruby didn't want to admit the only time she ever met someone so small was in the circus that came to the city once a year. After spending the next hour with the two, it became clear they were madly in love and well off.

Trying to ignore the hand holding and occasional kiss from the married couple, Ruby stared hard at the land outside as the sun began to fade from the sky. As the candle light came on in the train, its soft glow in the background helped to reflect the inside of the dining car through the glass window. A familiar reflection stood out.

Ruby stared, shocked and surprised. Sitting at a table with another couple was the thief, looking clean and dapper and enjoying a meal at her expense, no doubt. Not one to take action without thinking, Ruby realized she had two choices. She could march over to him and demand her stolen goods back or report him to the conductor and have him thrown off the train. Yet, without proof she would look like a fool and lose any chance of recovering her land certificates. No, she'd have to be more careful and find her property before she made any claims.

First, she needed to know if the couple at the table were his parents, mayhap she could take them aside and tell them what their son did. She slid the chair back and stood up. "If you will excuse me for a moment, I think I see someone I know."

Mr. and Mrs. Martin looked up and smiled before going right back to their conversation. They hardly took a second look. Ruby grinned at their dedication to one another. She hoped someday a man looked at her the way Mr. Martin looked at his wife. That's why she needed those land certificates back. She didn't care so much about the small amount of money in her reticule but the land certificates were her golden ticket.

She had to be careful how she approached the boy. Didn't need him running off scared and losing her only chance at making a new life for herself. Her mama explained how she could sell the certificates if need be or use them to purchase a parcel of land. In all fairness, she wanted to sell one for cash and use another one to buy a small parcel of land in Wichita Falls where she owned the place and no one could ever make her leave. She'd contract someone to build her a quaint log cabin and live happily ever after without a mean and nasty uncle to ruin her life. For now, she needed that boy.

"Good day. May I ask to join your conversation for a moment?" Ruby acknowledged the lady and directed herself to the man sitting across from the kid. She figured he was the head of the table.

"Ma'am." The gentleman pushed his chair back and stood up, nodding to her. "I assure you may. Please join us. What do we have the pleasure of your conversation for?"

"I thought I recognized this young fellow. I taught school in the city and at first it appeared he was one of my students. I wanted to come over and see if it was indeed one of my former students."

The gentleman's brow rose. "Do you know him? Seems he was all alone on the train, so my wife, Mrs. Carrington, deemed it suitable to escort the boy to his destination."

"I believe I do." Ruby made herself appear confused, as if she were trying to remember him. She directed her next conversation to the thief. "You were in my class last year. I'm just having a hard time recalling your name." She looked directly at the boy whose eyes were downcast. "It's Johnny, correct?"

The adults laughed. "No. He goes by William Dawson."

The kid began to fidget. He fiddled with his hands before hiding them under the white linen-clothed table. He wouldn't look at her.

Ruby threw her hands in the air, as if she now recalled everything. "You are correct, sir. He likes to be called Billy. I remember now." She turned to him, lowering herself gently to make eye contact. Except he wouldn't look up.

"He's a bit shy around the ears," Mr. Carrington mentioned.

"That's strange, the Billy I remember was quite the rambunctious type. Isn't that correct, Billy?"

There was no way he could avoid her. Politeness demanded he address the person talking to him, which happened to be Ruby. "Yes, ma'am," he mumbled, his eyes still downcast.

"Hello, Billy. I'm so glad to see you here. Where do you happen to be traveling all by yourself?"

"Oh, he's going to Wichita Falls to live with his uncle." Mrs. Carrington joined in the conversation, not letting Billy speak for himself. The two were nice to take him under their wings. Little did they know he was a pan handler and thief. "I wish we were heading that way, too, just to make sure he is deposited safely with his uncle. Unfortunately, we are getting off the train in the morning."

It was as if God had opened the heavens and showered good tidings. She shouldn't doubt Him, ever. Ruby placed a hand over her heart. "Oh! This is wonderful. I happen to be getting off at Wichita Falls myself. I'd be more than happy to escort my former student."

Mrs. Carrington smiled and clapped her gloved hands. "This is so wonderful. Thank you, Ms. Adams. It's highly kind of you to do so."

Ruby nodded. "It would be a pleasure. I must get back to my dinner companions but as soon as we are finished, I'll be back for Billy. He can ride next to me the remainder of the trip."

"Wonderful. Wonderful. We will see you then."

Ruby didn't miss the boy shuffling his feet back and forth under the table. She smiled as she worked her way back to the Martin's table. Her land certificates would be in her lap, along with her stolen reticule in a short while. She may as well enjoy the rest of her dinner.

Ruby snatched a look at the sleeping boy. Short, choppy blonde hair stuck out every which way, as if he hadn't had a proper haircut in ages. If she didn't know better, he looked like any other innocent kid. But there was a devil inside of him, that was for sure. She had to smile thinking about when she collected him in the dining car a few days ago. As they had walked away from the couple, he had tried to slip away but she grabbed him by the tip of his ear and marched him back to her seat in the passenger car. Since then, he had stayed put. Her threat to expose him for the lying thief he was had silenced him. She was sure he had the goods on him, it was why he complied.

He wasn't going anywhere until the train stopped at their destination, so she'd let him sleep. For now. In the meantime, Ruby slipped the rawhide tie from the small pile of worn letters. She stared at the writing. It was solid, strong and to be honest, the words popping out scared the daylights out of her. Why did the lady at the train station want her to read these?

Dear Catherine Jackson, thank you for returning my request for a mail order bride. My name is Marshall Montgomery. I own six hundred forty acres of raw land outside of Wichita Falls. Those who know me tell me I'm tall and handsome but I am an ordinary, hard working man who owns a herd of cattle, a few horses, and a small farm on the prairie. I'm looking for someone who works hard and can help me take care of my ten year old nephew, Billy. His parents died in a tragic carriage accident near their home in New York City. I'm sending for him to come live with me but I don't know how to take care of a child. I'm looking for someone who will help me care for my farm and keep the fires burning on the home front. If this sounds like something you are looking for, please write back. I need someone as soon as possible. I'm looking forward to hearing back from you real soon. Marshall Montgomery.

Ruby set the letter in her lap. Billy was this man's nephew? Why was the woman at the station holding letters from Billy's uncle? All of a sudden, Ruby realized the woman was supposed to go to Texas to mother this child. Why didn't she go? Did it have to do with the man who had been sitting next to her?

The boy had no parents to care for him. A touch of pity rose from deep inside until she pushed it right back down. The fact was Billy outright stole from her. How long had he been picking strangers pockets and why wasn't someone watching out for him? She opened the next letter, determined to get to the bottom of this confusing story.

"Dear Ms. Jackson,, Thanks for your letter. I'm sorry to read all about you having a fiancé who broke your heart and now all you wish to do is get far away from the big city life. You say you are a hard worker and that's what I need, someone to cook and clean and garden and be a mother to my nephew. If you'll be my mail order bride, I'll respect your wishes for marriage in name only until you can get over the heartbreak you have experienced. I am a busy man, so busy I'm planning to widen my horizons to buy more land. I won't have much time to dally with a wife. So if you would like to be my bride for a working relationship only, I've purchased a ticket for your trip to Wichita Falls, included in this letter. I'm afraid time is short, my nephew is on his way here. If you can't use the ticket, please return it to me and I will understand. Marshall Montgomery.

The realization hit Ruby so hard she gasped. She was given the ticket for the train ride as a swap for a mail order bride. The woman, Catherine, stayed in New York City. The man beside her on the bench was no doubt her fiancé, who came to the station to stop her from marrying someone else. A story out of the pages of a romantic penny novel. She let the paper fall to her lap and closed her eyes.

She had sold her soul without realizing what she did. The woman at the station saw her desperation and used it to her advantage. Not that she didn't blame the lady for staying with her true love but that left Ruby in a terrible situation.

"Why are you pretending to be Catherine Jackson?"

The tiny voice startled Ruby. She opened her eyes and turned to Billy. He held the letter she dropped. A tiny smile landed on his face as if he knew she was guarding a secret. "Who says I'm pretending to be anyone?" Ruby shot back.

"You have these letters from my uncle. That means you are his mail order bride. What's a mail order bride?" The curiosity of a ten year old almost made Ruby smile. Almost. She was still furious at the kid for his thievery, even if she did kind of understand why he had behaved so badly.

"It's hard to explain to a child."

"You said your name is Ruby Adams. You told those people that's your name."

"Give me my reticule and I'll tell you."

The boy shuffled his feet, twisting his fingers in his lap. "I don't have it any more."

Ruby's heart skipped a beat.

"What do you mean you don't have it? That is my life. I need the land certificates! You can keep the money, just give me the papers."

The boy stared. His face paled. "I threw the reticule out the window when I saw you on the train."

"What!" Ruby stuttered. Her eyes widened in shock. She wanted to wrap her hands around the boy's throat and shake him. Everything was lost. A sudden hysteria almost freed itself from somewhere deep inside. She'd have to become a mail order bride now just to survive. There was no going back, no other options, no begging her uncle to take her in. She wouldn't do what her mother did and beg for a home. No. She'd find a way out of this mess.

"I did take some old papers out before I threw it out the window. 'Cause they looked important."

She stared at the boy. Relief flooded through every single orifice of Ruby's body. She swiped at her brow with a shaky hand before holding out an open palm. "Give me the papers."

His small head shook back and forth. It was plain to see he was scared, yet he held his own. The little conniving thief was going to hold them from her. What did he want?

"Billy, I'm warning you. I know you have the papers on you. I'll call the conductor over here to turn you upside down and shake you until those papers fall out of your person. Then you'll go to jail for stealing. Or, have some fingers cut off."

Billy stiffened. "They don't cut off fingers, do they?" He shrank back in his seat. Trying to be a street-smart tough kid was taking its toll. Billy was a troubled boy caught up in a bad situation. Ruby didn't want him to be scared but she wanted her property back.

"I hear they do awful things out here in the wild west. Men get hung from a tree for stealing a horse. Imagine what they would do to a boy who stole from a lady!"

The boy's eyes widened in stark fear. "Who's they? Are their people here on the train who'll hang me?"

Ruby decided to be honest with him. "Not really. I'm going to bargain with you, Billy. If you give me my papers back, I'll forget you ever stole my reticule and won't press charges. It will be our secret. Agreed?" She turned to him and held out a hand, trying to gain his trust. After all, knowing his story, she was pretty certain he had no one to look out for him. It was probably why he was running loose in the city. Going to the uncle's farm was the best thing to straighten him out. She wouldn't have him punished for a mistake. Everyone made them. Ruby wanted to forgive and forget and move on. With her land certificates. She would turn one in for the cash and pay the uncle for the ticket after explaining why she couldn't marry him. It was all starting to work itself out for the good of all involved.

The boy's hand stilled. He didn't remove it from his lap. His little blonde head lifted up to look her dead in the eye. "There's no one on the train to hang me?"

Ruby let a sly smile escape. "Of course not, Billy. I was trying to scare you. I'll have my papers back, please. It's time for us to move on."

"Well then, I think I will bargain, too."

She glared at him. The innocent look left his face as quick as silver. "What do you mean you will bargain with me? I'm not the one who stole anything?"

"In a way you did."

"What! Billy, give me those papers, right now!"

"Is there a problem here, Miss?" the attendant asked, standing over the two of them.

She waved him away. "Not at all. Billy here told me some surprising news."

"Good day, Ma'am." The attendant tipped his hat and moved on to another passenger.

Billy puffed out his chest before he sat back in his seat and smiled. "The way I see it, if I give you the papers, you can turn me in and have me hanged. There's no way around things now. I'll have to keep them hidden until I'm safe with my uncle."

"You little brat!"

Chapter 4

The attendant cupped his hands over his mouth. "Two minutes until Wichita Falls. If you look to the North, you can see the town in all its glory."

The chatter of passengers excited voices rang in Ruby's ears. She turned on the boy. "You give me my papers right now, you little conniving thief!" Billy was using her generosity and turning on her.

He crossed his arms over his chest and shook his little head back and forth. "No."

"Billy, don't make me tell your uncle what you did."

"Don't make me tell him you aren't Catherine Jackson."

"Why, you, little," she stopped. Ruby wouldn't get anywhere this way. She knew by the stoic look on his face he would play this part until he deemed safe.

"Little what?" he dared.

Even though she was seething inside, Ruby raised her hand and patted him on the head, maybe a little harder than necessary. "You win. I'll be patient and play the part of Catherine Jackson until you decide I'm trustworthy enough to give those papers back. I'll keep your secret safe so your uncle won't know what a little, low-down, conniving trouble-maker you are." She held out her hand. "Deal?"

He giggled at her description of him. "Deal." The boy was clearly loving every moment of this. Oh, she'd show him a thing or two after they settled in at his uncle's house. She'd wait until no one was about and shake him upside down and retrieve those papers and be on her way to finding her own land and place in society. Some little smart-mouthed kid wasn't going to stop her from making her dreams come true.

She had to admit he was clever. The boy wasn't taking any chances and even though it affected her, Ruby was an adult. She'd find her way out of this mess but for a kid it had to be harder. She had to admire his gumption in the dire situation he was placed in. Even so, pretending to be Marshall Montgomery's intended wife would give her some time to look over Wichita Falls and see where she wanted to stake a land claim. After all, it wasn't as if the man were looking for a real bride. He wanted someone to take care of the kid. It wouldn't be a big deal to run off when she got her land certificates back.

The train came to a halt, its steam engine making so much noise Ruby held her ears closed. When others began to abandon their seats to depart, Ruby nodded for Billy to go first. She wasn't about to let him out of her sight. Not now, not ever, or, at least until she got her belongings back. She eyed him from the top of his head to the tips of his boots to see where he would hide them, but there was no way she could get him to empty his pockets.

Ruby pulled her bonnet to shade her eyes so she could get an overall picture of Wichita Falls. The small town was charming, a bit dusty but she recognized the odd buildings cluttering both sides of main street. A mercantile, saloon, livery and even a church stood tall and proud against the blue and white sky of the prairie. The wind blew straw and tumbleweeds across the dusty street where they rolled over and over across the dying grass. It wasn't a bustling city like New York, far from it but Ruby needed a new place to live. Perhaps this was where she would find home.

Standing on the platform of the train depot, she hugged her piece of luggage a bit closer. Her other hand was in Billy's clammy one as he clung to her as if she were his savior. After what he did, she'd like to squeeze those fingers until he handed over her property.

A tall man stood at the end of the depot, a cowboy hat in his hand. Thick dark hair was a tad longer than most but it did something for his looks. He seemed more like an outlaw instead of a rancher. With a gunbelt slung low on his hip, Ruby couldn't help but take a quick glance at his physique. He was a handsome man. She knew without a doubt he was Marshall Montgomery.

She squeezed Billy's hand without thinking. "Ouch," he whispered, squirming like a fish out of water. "Ruby! Stop squeezing me!"

The man's quick response shocked Ruby. He was no slouch in the smarts department. "Ruby? I suppose you aren't the person I'm looking for, then. But, the little fellow there, I know he's my sister's child. He looks just like her. Welcome home, Billy."

Billy took a step forward. He acted as if he wanted to run towards the man and fling himself in his uncle's arms. Except he didn't. He began to bite his lower lip. He was a scared little boy who lost his mama and papa and now had to go to a strange place to grow up.

It was plain to Ruby the man noticed too. "It's fine, Billy. You won't come to no harm with me. I have a nice ranch a ways from here. Do you like to ride horses?"

Billy nodded. "I ain't never saw any up close except for the ones pulling carts down the street."

The man clearly knew how to handle the boy. He knelt on one knee, bringing himself more to the boy's level. "Well, come on then. I have a ranch full of horses and cows who will be needing your help." There was something about watching a man like Marshall Montgomery with a small boy that made her think it may not be so bad married to someone like him. She shook herself. Thoughts like that wouldn't do her any good.

Billy slowly let go of her hand. She felt the air between them and realized he would soon be gone. Since Marshall Montgomery didn't think she was his intended bride, she would be homeless and helpless in a strange town. Without any money!

She couldn't let Billy get away!

As the boy began to walk towards Marshall, she noticed how the man looked out over the area, his eyes roving around as if looking for someone else. A shudder went through her as she realized he was looking for his mail order bride. "I am Catherine Jackson," she spoke up quickly as the lie slipped from her mouth.

Billy grinned.

Marshall fixed dark eyes on her. "I heard the boy call you Ruby. I'm looking for one Catherine Jackson from New York City."

She stared right back, her intentions only to get her land certificates back. "I am Catherine, also known as Ruby, which is my preferred name, here to meet one Marshall Montgomery to become his mail order bride. In name only," she added, glad she had taken the time to read the letters. It gave her more insight on how to behave. This Catherine was a heartbroken woman who was here to heal from a lost love. Would she be able to pull this off until the boy came through for her?

When she told him in name only, he appeared relieved. His brow rose and he nodded. "You said nothing about a Ruby." His narrowed eyes spoke of a man who wanted the truth.

She shuddered. He wouldn't be happy when she broke their engagement, even though it couldn't be helped. She wasn't about to marry anyone. Not ever. Not until she made her lot in life and had enough land and money to be an independent woman. Like her Aunt Adeline. Ruby never wanted to be beholden to anyone.

Mayhap she should tell this man the truth and make the boy pay for his sins. Then she could take her land certificates, get some advice from her aunt and be done with this mess. Except, if she disclosed the truth, the boy may well be sent back to New York. To what? To a life of crime he was sure to be faced with without anyone to supervise him. No, she wasn't that cruel. The boy needed a chance, a new life to grow and become the man God intended him to be. Her own mother gave her a good life regardless of her cruel uncle. She had even sacrificed her own happiness to do so. When she looked at the way Billy held on to the rancher's hand, her heart did a flip.

"My full name is Catherine Ruby Jackson. It was also my mother's name so my father called me Ruby so as not to get us confused. I use it only with my dear friends and family."

Marshall watched as she tried to explain, his face amused. Did he know she was lying? When he grinned, she let out the breath she was holding. "Well, then, I suppose we should go see Daniel Conners."

Ruby let him take her only piece of luggage and place it in a wagon sitting along the side of the train depot. She followed him down the wooden board walk, holding up her skirts so as not to get the edges full of mud. Marshall took her elbow and guided her in to the Parish office, Billy not far behind.

"Daniel," Marshall announced. "We're mostly ready to get this moving along."

A cold fear hit Ruby in the middle of her gut. She looked at Billy first, then Marshall. "Move what along?"

He shrugged. "Why, our marriage. I explained in the last letter when you get here, Daniel will have everything ready to go. No sense in waiting since it's a marriage of convenience only. The sooner the boy has a new mother, the quicker we can get settled in and he can get started living his new life on the farm. I have a cattle drive next week and can't leave this boy alone."

Ruby didn't think to read to the end of the letter. "But, I thought, well, I wanted to wait a bit," Ruby spit out, jumbling words that made no sense. This wasn't supposed to happen. She couldn't marry a man like Marshall Montgomery!

Billy giggled. "Will I be able to call her mommie?" he asked Marshall, a grin spreading from ear to ear.

Marshall lowered himself back down to Billy's level. "If she agrees, I think eventually you may want to. That doesn't mean you will forget yours. She'll always be in here." Marshall placed a large hand over the boy's heart.

Ruby couldn't speak. How could she marry a man she didn't love or even know? For one, if she did marry him, she'd be tied to him forever. Her land certificates wouldn't do her any good then, they'd be his by rights. She would be stuck on a farm, working hard for someone else, living with a man who wanted no love in his life, just a woman who worked herself to the bone. Which she didn't mind hard work but this was not why she came out west. She turned to Billy, who stood beside Marshall snickering.

A sudden thought occurred when Ruby got her head on straight. She was marrying this man as Catherine Jackson, not Ruby Adams. Therefore, there was no marriage to end. No one would ever know if she took her land certificates and moved on from here. She could pull this off. She would have to leave this small town but that was okay. There was land to be had all over the west, it didn't mean it had to be right here. Nine chances out of ten, she'd never run into Marshall Montgomery after today.

Ruby had to make some amends and change her plan of action. Marshall Montgomery was staring at her, hard. As if she were expected to say something. Next, the boy looked up, his guilty little eyes staring at her in amusement. The man he called Daniel held open a bible. He smiled at Ruby.

She was expected to say something but what had they asked of her? "I'm sorry, I guess I'm a bit nervous," she told them, taking a step back.

"It's not unusual ma'am," Daniel told her. "I just need you to agree to become Marshall's wife so we can wrap this up."

The three of them stared at her, waiting.

"I, well, yes. Yes, I do." *At least Catherine does.*

Marshall sighed. She didn't miss the fact his shoulders relaxed at her words.

"I now pronounce you man and wife, you may kiss your bride."

Kiss his bride! Oh, dear!

Marshall moved towards her, the look of intent on his face taking her breath away. Ruby wasn't sure she would recover from a kiss by him. He was not what she had expected, although she had no idea what she expected. Certainly not such a handsome, fine man like him.

He placed warm hands on her shoulders. She stared at one of them, noticing the large calloused hands. Yet they were soft to the touch. A hard working man, yet gentle, stirred her insides even more.

Closing her eyes, she puckered her lips. She waited for a moment for him to kiss her. When she didn't feel anything against her mouth, her eyes flickered open to see him right there, inches from her face. He was staring in to her very soul. Did he see her deceit? Shame showered down on her, almost forcing her to take a step back but his large hands held her there. He dipped his head and kissed her.

Oh, sweet Jesus, thank you! The man was a gift from above. The soft, gentle way he placed his mouth on hers stirred every inch of her into oblivion. She should push him away but instead, Ruby grabbed his shirt to pull him closer.

The preacher cleared his throat.

Ruby stepped back, pushing herself away from this man. "I'm sorry," she whispered, not sure what had gotten in to her.

"Perfectly fine, Mrs. Montgomery. The two of you are married, allowed to have a kiss in public." The preacher looked at his own wife, who stood beside him. "We certainly don't need any fireworks," he teased in a low voice.

Ruby was so shaken up she didn't recall how she wound up an hour later riding shotgun on a wagon bench with the boy between the two of them. Marshall had the reins wrapped around his powerful hands. He gazed over at her when he saw her staring. "Everything alright, Mrs. Montgomery?"

"Fine," she got out, then turned to the prairie. The kiss had shaken her up. She never expected to feel anything. There was something between the two of them, for sure. This could develop in to a problem. She wasn't supposed to feel anything for the man. No, she was going to get to the ranch and turn the kid upside down for her land certificates and flee before anyone knew she was missing.

Ruby bit her lip. Her plan didn't sound like it would work too well. Not with a man like Montgomery. He was too keen, to strong and too, well, too kissable.

"Penny for your thoughts?" he asked.

She turned back to him, avoiding looking in to his beautiful eyes. "I'm anxious to see your home, that's all."

"It's right over yonder," he told her, pointing ahead of the wagon with the reins. Looking ahead, there was miles and miles of barren land. Marshall turned down a dirt path. "It sets way back but you can see the outline of the barn and house over there."

Twenty minutes later they were in the yard, looking at a towering two story house and barn. "It's nice,"she told him, hiking up her skirts and jumping off the wagon before he could help her. A frown appeared on his face when he noticed she didn't wait for his help, but he didn't say a word.

He would have to get used to her independent spirit, she mused. That is, until she left here. Taking the steps two at a time, Ruby flung open the door to find a large space filled with a long table and some wooden benches, along with a few chairs scattered about. A cook stove set in the corner, along with space to do some serious preparations. On the other side of the room, several rockers were lined up around a fireplace. It was cozy yet there wasn't a woman's touch here at all.

That would change if she had any say in the décor. Of course, she wouldn't be here long enough to make a difference.

"Does it suit?" Marshall stood beside her.

"It's nice. Needs a woman's touch."

"I give you full rein to do as you will."

He was a nice man. She felt a tinge of regret to lead him on this way. Taking a deep breath, she let it out slowly. "I think it's fine for now. I'd like to get started with the meal if you don't mind."

"Everything is in the kitchen," he told her, pointing towards another door leading outside. "There are potatoes in the root cellar right out back and we finished building the smoke house over yonder. If you need anything, ask Joe, he's been doing the cooking for some time now."

"Thank you. Where do I find Joe?" she asked, shyly stepping back from his towering physique.

"Out in the barn, mucking the stalls this time of day while the horses are gone. He's an all around cowboy, does the cooking, keeps the ranch in shape. I'm sure he'll be happy now that you're here to take over some of the work."

Oh brother! Ruby smiled but turned away before he could see the lies all over her face. Setting to work, she grabbed an iron to stir the embers in the fireplace in the kitchen, bringing them to life. When she had a good fire going, Ruby looked over the shelves to find something to cook for their dinner.

Marshall stood at the door, his hand on the knob. "When supper is ready, you can ring the bell out here on the porch. We'll all be up for dinner in no time flat."

"We?" she questioned. How many people was she supposed to feed?

As if he could read her mind, he said, "There's five of us, six with me, plus you and the boy. Good day, Mrs. Montgomery."

Ruby sighed. There wasn't a whole lot of variety on the shelves, which was so unlike the pantry in their brownstone. Even though her uncle had a cook, her mama made Ruby cook and clean over the years, too. She never wanted her daughter to be idle. Right now, she was glad her mother took the initiative to teach her. Otherwise, Marshall would see her for the fake she was and probably throw her out on her own in the middle of the Texas prairie.

She ventured out back and found the door to the root cellar, and worked her way down the three rickety steps. Walking across the ground dirt floor, Ruby couldn't help darting her eyes back and forth for rodents or anything that may be hiding in the dark corners. Holding open her apron that she put on from the hook on the kitchen door, Ruby gathered enough potatoes for a large pot of stew. Feeding more than a few people would be difficult but she would do her best.

Back in the kitchen, she began to clean the skins of the potatoes, before cutting them up and placing them in the pot to stew. Looking out of the kitchen window, Ruby smiled. Two full-grown apple trees, along with some she wasn't sure what they were, stood in the yard, big and tall and proud. One thing she did know how to make was a wicked apple pie. Even her uncle would rave about the delicious taste whenever she did the baking. She'd find some good apples and throw in a pie or two for desert. That way when she did leave here, perhaps he'd remember that she wasn't all that bad.

Ruby set about gathering carrots, onions and other vegetables from the garden to add to her stew. Then she shook a few of the branches of the apple tree until plenty fell on the ground and commenced to make her apple pie. Before long, the hours flew by and it was time to call them in for supper.

Ruby cleaned herself up the best she could and went outside to ring the big iron bell hanging from the porch. She moved the makeshift cord back and forth, the bell filling the air with a loud noise. Men came out of nowhere, yelling *suppers done* before taking the few steps to the back door of the kitchen. Ruby watched from her place on the wooden porch until each man went through the kitchen door. She had set up the table earlier, pushing two benches along each side of the table for them to sit down together.

As she looked around, she didn't see the boy or Marshall so went inside to help serve supper. "Where's Mr. Montgomery?"

"Boss said to go ahead and serve supper, he'll be along in a while. Seems a cow that strayed is having trouble bearing her calf. Him and the boy are out there now. It'll be a few hours until they get back. Said to save him some supper."

Joe lifted the Dutch oven from the fireplace. "I've done this before, ma'am. I'll help to serve supper if you want to get to cutting the pie on the windowsill."

Ruby was glad for his help. Joe was a large man, strong hands and a smile that helped put her at ease. She wasn't sure how to feel having so many men at the table but they all seemed harmless enough. She was sure a man like Marshall wouldn't allow them inside if he didn't trust them.

Joe ladled stew for each man. As he sat down and crossed his hand over his chest, a small prayer was heard by one of the men. Then they picked up their spoons and began to dig in to the meal. One by one, each man's eyes looked at Ruby.

Finally, one of the men stared at her, disapproval on his hard-lined face. "Where in tarnation is the meat?"

Chapter 5

Ruby's hand stilled. "The what?"

Another ranch hand chimed in. "The meat! We have a smoke house out back here filled with meat. We want meat with our supper, no offense ma'am."

Ruby's face paled. Oh darn, she had forgotten to put meat in the stew. With all the things she had been doing, she meant to go to the smoke house and grab a ham for the pot of stew. She bit her bottom lip. They were going to think she was incompetent if she didn't clear this up. Then Marshall would make her leave and she'd have to leave her land certificates behind. At that very moment she wanted to shake the boy. He was the cause of all this distress. "I'm sorry, but I thought you'd like my special Potato Soup for tonight. I didn't have a lot of time to cook and I wanted to concentrate on this special pie." She held up the pie, it's rich aroma filling the air. The men were silent for some time, staring at the pie in her hands.

"Well, alright. We'll take pie then instead of meat." The others nodded their heads and agreed. Ruby didn't hesitate but served them each a large slice. She even poured some fresh milk in their mugs.

"Now that's right fine of you, ma'am. Thank you and sorry for demanding meat. This is indeed a fine supper."

"Anything's better than the slop Joe was cookin' for us. A hard-working man gets tired of beans every single night."

Joe snickered. "If I never see a Dutch oven again, I'll be a happy man."

She smiled at the banter and nodded as each man thanked her for the meal. They left the kitchen one by one until she was left all alone. Ruby began to clean up, wondering where in the world Marshall and Billy were at. The sky was darkening. Was it safe to be out on the plains at night?

She kept the stew warm in the corner of the fireplace, away from direct heat so it didn't dry out. The pie was still warm but it wouldn't stay that way much longer. Should she be worried they weren't back yet?

Ruby went outside on the back porch to find two rocking chairs sitting beside the other, facing the prairie. She lowered herself on to one of the chairs and began to rock back and forth, its lull causing her to drift off. When she stirred awake, the sky was so dark it frightened her. She stood up. Dare she go in to the barn? It was a ways from the house, she could stumble and fall in the dark night.

It looked like the bunkhouse sat beside the barn. Ruby could make out a faint light in the window. No one else seemed concerned. Should she be? She didn't want to bother anyone and yet what if Marshall didn't come back? Or the boy? Maybe someone should go looking for them.

Besides, her land certificates were on that boy and if anything happened to him, she'd never be free to live a life as an independent woman. She breathed in the clean night air. It was fresh, not like the city smells of dust and factory toils, garbage in the streets and other smells she'd be ashamed to name. A girl like Ruby could get used to living on a ranch. Perhaps she'd even have one of her own some day. If everything worked out right. Worry began to cover her brow. Not just for her land certificates but she was starting to worry a little bit about the two out on the prairie. How could that be in such a short amount of time?

She decided to wait on the porch, so sat back down in the rocker, since he never told her where she'd be sleeping. Ruby didn't even know if she'd have her own bedroom or be stuck with Marshall. Chills went through her spine thinking about being in the same bed with him. After all, they were married now but she had no plans to make it a permanent position. He was married to one Catherine Jackson. Ruby Adams was still a single woman.

Ruby took her fingertips and rubbed her aching forehead. She began to rock back and forth until it seemed as if everything faded away in to the dark of the night.

<><>

Marshall tried to explain to Billy how cows are born but he was a city boy. He'd never had to experience anything like this before. The fascination and stark fear on his face when the cow began her labor made him chuckle. The boy had a lot of learning to do. "You gonna throw up, boy?" he asked, amused.

Billy was on his knees beside the cow as she began to make painful noises. Mostly she was quiet but in these last stages of labor it was getting harder. "No, sir. I can take it," he told his uncle.

Marshall grinned. Wait until he had to see what was about to happen. "I'm afraid you may want to turn your head, son."

The boy stared at him before shaking his head. "I can take it, Uncle Marshall."

As the cow screamed, Marshall did the only thing he could to help her. He had to move the calf so it could be born. He pushed his arm inside to pull the hoofs out of the mother. It was difficult and sweat poured from his brow. It wasn't the first time he'd had to do this but he hated to watch her suffer. Hopefully, the calf would be born alive and the ailing mother would survive.

A few minutes of pulling and the calf slipped from its mother, covered in slimy liquid. Marshall looked up to see the petrified look on Billy's face. "Do I have to ever do that?" he whispered, horrified.

"Maybe so, son. It just saved this mama's life."

"It did?" He sat back on his haunches as if in deep thought. "Well, then, I'll do it too if I have to. I know what it's like to lose a mommy. I'm glad she didn't die."

His words were so profound it took Marshall a moment to recover. This ranch would be good for the boy. Even though he was sad his parents were gone, there was nothing like hard work to help recover from tragedy. "Let's back up a bit," Marshall told the boy as he stepped away from mother and baby.

They watched silently as the mother's tongue slaked out and licked the calf from head to foot then nudged the calf on its feet. The newborn wobbled on shaky legs for sometime before lifting herself up like a trooper, searching for food. She stood there, wobbling until she found her prize and began suckling.

Marshall began to gather branches and limbs from the area for a fire. "Son, we're going to have to stay here and protect the mother and baby tonight. Do you think you can do that?"

He nodded, excitement in his next words. "Like a shepherd watching over the sheep?" he asked, his ten year old voice sounding loud and proud.

"That's right, just like a shepherd." While Marshall got a fire going, he pulled his saddlebags and two blankets from the horse. They didn't have much of a choice, really. If a pack of wolves happened by, the mother and baby would die. Marshall couldn't afford to lose any of his cattle. They would stand guard tonight and run them closer to the ranch at first signs of daylight. He wasn't sure how this one slipped away so far from the ranch, but sometimes it happened.

After settling in, Marshall laid on his back, a rifle by his side. He looked up at the sky, a few stars twinkling in the darkness. He wondered what Catherine was doing right now? She sure was beautiful, except there was an air of mystery about her he wasn't so sure about. She sure didn't seem like a heartbroken woman who was jilted by her fiancé. Marshall had a feeling in his gut there was something else going on. He kicked some dirt from the tip of his boot.

When Billy called her Ruby instead of Catherine, he thought it strange at first. He was certain she wasn't his intended. Later, when she had admitted she was indeed Catherine, claiming to be Catherine Ruby Jackson, he saw the twinge of fear on her face before she shielded it behind that sweet smile. He sighed, taking in the night air deep in his lungs.

There was also something strange about the boy, too. He just couldn't put a finger on it. Yet. Billy kept pulling up his pant leg, checking for something in his shoe. When Marshall told him he'd have to trade those shoes in for a pair of cowboy boots, the kid took a step back in fear as if Marshall would take the shoes from him right then and there. He assured the boy he'd have to wait to get a new pair when they went back in town next. The look of relief on the boy's face made Marshall wonder why a kid his age wouldn't want to trade his city shoes for a fine pair of boots. What was he hiding in those shoes?

Between the woman and the boy, Marshall had a feeling his hands were full. He'd have to keep them both in his line of vision.

<><>

Marshall saw the ranch house in the distance. The morning dew on the tips of the grass sparkled like little crystals. He guided his stallion to the barn, then slipped the boy off the saddle to carry him to the house. Billy was out like a rock after stargazing for hours last night. He had refused to fall asleep, taking Marshall's words seriously that they had to keep watch all night. He didn't expect the boy to stay awake, but he did anyway, earning respect from Marshall.

The closer he got to the house, Marshall noticed Catherine asleep on the rocking chair on the porch. Had she been there all night waiting? A small feeling arose from deep inside but he squelched it back down. Wouldn't do any good to stir up anything. She was here for one reason. He slipped past her in to the house and took the steps two at a time to deposit the boy on the feather mattress in the small upstairs bedroom.

When Marshall went back out on the porch, he stood for a moment watching his new wife sleep. She sure was a mystery. His heart tugged for a moment realizing she still wore an apron around her waist. There were traces of corn meal on her cheek as she slept away. Her head lolled to one side then her eyelashes blinked a few times before those blue eyes were staring at him.

She shot out of the chair like an Indian on the warpath. "I'm so sorry, I fell asleep."

Marshall smiled. Were you out here all night?" he asked, even though he knew it to be true.

"I was worried. Where's the boy?" She looked around, frantic, as if it was her own son she searched for.

He thought that odd. She didn't seem to like the boy all that much when they rode in on the wagon yesterday. "Upstairs. Asleep. He was up all night guarding a newly born calf."

She smiled, wringing her hands. "That explains things. I'll start breakfast." She went to walk past him when he stopped her with a hand to her wrist.

"If you would like to get some rest, I'll show you where you will be sleeping." She stiffened, like she were afraid he would make a pass at her. He had no plans, now, or in the future, to bed the woman. She was his wife in name only, they had established the terms through the letters. But why did he feel so charged and want to bend his head to kiss her right this moment?

"I, I'm fine. I slept throughout the night. The men will be up for breakfast before long. I better get started."

Since when did she take such an interest in his men? He didn't ask, but nodded instead. He pushed his hands deep in his pockets as he leaned against the porch railing as she walked by. Marshall went in to the house to show her where her bedroom would be. Their bedroom.

Marshall hadn't thought things through enough. The boy had the upstairs room. The day he sent a ticket for the boy, he had put a bed there. He didn't think ahead to where his bride would sleep. Now he wondered if he would be able to keep his hands off of her sharing the same room. She was so lovely. Incredibly so. He opened the solid oak door. "The boy has the upstairs room, this will be yours."

He stood behind her in the center of the room, noticing the moment she spotted a pair of his britches hanging from the hook on the inside of the door. Another shirt was flung carelessly on a rocker by the fireplace. Even though it wasn't often they saw cold weather, there were chilly nights at times. Many times when Marshall would come in off the ranch, he'd sit in front of the fire and fall asleep staring at those flames. Too exhausted to crawl in bed, there were plenty of times he'd get back up and continue his day. But that was what helped build his ranch, little sleep and lots of work.

It was starting to pay off.

"It looks as if this room is taken." His new bride stared at his clothes, her brow raised.

He nodded. "I can sleep in the bunkhouse." He wasn't too fond of sleeping with a bunch of other men but if that was what she wanted, he would do so to keep everyone happy. Besides, he didn't know if he could keep his hands to himself if he were sharing a bed with her. The reality of everything hit him hard.

She shook her head. "No, I refuse to move you out of your own bed. We can share. It may be difficult but we are man and wife. How would it look to the others if you slept there?"

"Good point. Although it's none of anyone's business what I do. I can take the upstairs room with the boy."

"Nonsense. How will that look to him? He's confused enough. I'll take the room with the boy."

"The bed isn't big enough for two. It would be easier for me to take a bedroll and fall asleep on the floor beside his bed."

His new bride placed a hand on either side of her hips. He liked the way she pulled her shoulders back and flung her chin in the air. "Nonsense, I say. We will sleep here as man and wife, in name only and the boy gets the room upstairs. I know you are an honorable man and will keep your word that this marriage is in name only. That way there won't be any harm and when I'm gone," she said before going silent. Her eyes widened and she shook her head.

"Gone? You going somewhere?"

Her face paled. "No." She turned quickly to head out the door. "I have breakfast to start." The swish of her hips distracted him for a moment before her words hit him full force.

Now he knew more than ever that something was going on. It had to do with her and the boy.

He sighed, knowing he had to get to the bottom of things before leaving on the cattle drive. Marshall didn't want to come back to an empty house. Not even after one day.

He kind of liked a woman here.

Chapter 6

Ruby let out the breath she was holding. Being in the same small space with a man like Marshall was intoxicating. Stirring the coals to life, she placed a cast iron pan over the fire. Time to forget about his distracting ways and make the men their meal.

Staring in to the fire, she realized what she almost said. Ruby had to be careful. If he found out she was a fraud, he'd throw her out on her ear. He was such a nice man, honest to the core. "I doubt I have to worry about my honor," she mumbled to herself, wondering why that seemed to disappoint her. It was because of the kiss at the alter, the one which stirred her soul to the very core. She had never, ever been kissed like that before, not by a long shot. Ruby touched her lips with her fingertips, as if she could still feel his mouth on her own.

"Everything alright?" his voice asked from behind her. He stood too close, only a breath's inch away. She didn't dare turn around, else she'd be in his arms. She nodded. This had to stop. Ruby was so glad when footsteps pounded on the outside porch and the kitchen door opened. A whoosh of cool morning air tumbled across the room.

"Mornin' bossman, Misses bossman," Max mumbled.

She noticed the moment Marshall stepped away. It was as if the cold air surrounded her, leaving her empty. Ruby gritted her teeth. She wasn't supposed to feel this way. Not about this man. *Get yourself together, girl. Get a hold of yourself and concentrate on the paperwork you need!*

Turning to the men, she plastered a smile on her face. "Good morning, Max. Breakfast will be ready shortly. Please, have a seat." Ruby kept her back to the men as she prepared pancakes, along with warm maple syrup and a tub of churned butter. Slowly, as if they were dragged out of bed, the other men filed in one by one, yawning and dragging their boots across the kitchen floor.

The pleasant sounds of their moans as they ate her fluffy pancakes pleased Ruby. She had cooked plenty of times at home, but these men were so appreciate. It made her feel all warm inside. As if she found a place where she was wanted and needed. She quickly turned back to the task at hand. Wanting to please even more, Ruby began to kneed the bread for tonight's supper. She planned to have plenty of meat and some warm, thick bread for the evening meal. Taking a deep breath, she had to stop this nonsense. Although they were all happy for the food she made, it wouldn't do any good for them to get used to having a woman around, since she wasn't sticking around here very long.

"Uncle Marshall?" Billy rubbed his eyes as his shoes pitter-pattered over the wooden floor.

"Morning."

Ruby turned to the boy. "Morning, Billy."

He flashed her a quick look and grinned, his sleepy eyes looking so innocent. But she knew he wasn't. She glanced at his clothes, looking him up and down to see where he hid the papers.

Another grin flashed her way.

Ruby turned away. The little thief was about to have his world turned upside down. She had to get him alone. Some how, some way. Today she was going to get the paperwork and be on her way. It wouldn't do her any good to get too used to this place.

The boy sat at the table with the others, scarfing up the pancakes as though he hadn't eaten in ages. She turned to watch him throw another pancake on his plate and drown the thick cake in maple syrup. A secret smile crossed her face. She was trying not to like the kid.

Marshall finished his meal and slid back his plate. He leaned back on his chair. "Billy, you ready to go in to town today? It looks like you are in need of a pair of cowboy boots."

Billy stopped chewing. He glanced at his feet. Ruby didn't miss a thing. "Right now?" he asked, desperation in his tone.

"As soon as the wagon is ready to go. I need some supplies for the cattle drive next week. Thought you may want to trade those shoes in for a real pair of boots. You'll need them to help Ruby with the chores while I'm gone."

The boy didn't look too good. His face paled and he mumbled something before shoving the rest of the pancake in his mouth. "I'll be right back," he tried to say before leaving the table to run back up the stairs.

"Now what in tarnation got in to that boy?" Marshall asked, a line of confusion on his brow.

Ruby didn't say a word. She knew exactly what was wrong. The little liar and thief had her land certificates in his shoes. Now she understood why he was always patting his leg and feet. A slow smile cracked her cheeks. She knew exactly what to do. As soon as they got to town, she would offer to take the boy for his boots. Once he got those shoes off, she would take back her property and make plans to be on her way to a new life.

Frantic, she began to clean up breakfast as the men left one by one. "Don't leave without me," Ruby told Marshall, who was still at the table reading a local gazette.

"You want to go in to town with us?" His brow raised, she could feel his stare on her back.

She nodded. "Yes, I'd like to pick up a few things myself, if you don't mind?"

"Yes, of course. Anything you want, Ruby. Put it on my account."

It was that easy? She grinned, finishing up the dishes and placing two pieces of cloth she found over top of the pans of yeast to let it rise. Tonight would be another delicious meal for the men, with meat this time and fresh bread. A smile curved her lips as she placed the apron she wore back on the hook by the door. How wonderful it felt to be needed. Then Billy came back in to the room and she remembered why she was here in the first place.

<><>

It wasn't far to town but the road was bumpy. Marshall held the reins in his strong hands. Ruby's eyes were fixed on those strong hands, determining she would miss them. And him. How could she begin to like someone so much in a days time? Perhaps if he would be a mean man like her uncle, she wouldn't have any trouble at all. The fact was he was truly a nice person.

Billy fidgeted in the back of the wagon. "Uncle Marshall, how long will you be on the cattle drive? Can I go along? I know how to help if a cow has a baby?"

A smile flickered across Marshall's face. He clicked his tongue and nudged the horses to go a bit faster. "Not this time, son. I really need you at the ranch. Who will take care of Mrs. Montgomery while I'm gone?"

"I can take care of my own," she began then stopped when he looked at her with a raised brow. Sorry, she mouthed, realizing he was trying to let the boy down easy, trying to make him feel needed. "Actually, I need someone to show me how to milk the cows and to gather eggs. I don't know how to, Billy."

Billy smirked. "That's silly. Anyone knows how to get eggs from the hens."

"Not me," she told him. "I'm from the city, remember? Never had to deal with those horrible chickens. They squawk and carry on, I doubt anyone will have eggs if you let it up to me."

"Uncle Marshall showed me how to gather the eggs first thing yesterday. I guess I can try to teach you." The seriousness of his voice made her look at Marshall, who was grinning.

She tried to stifle a laugh. Of course she knew how to gather eggs, but it made him feel needed instead.

"You'll stay and help out at the ranch, and by the time the next cattle drive comes along, you can help me, okay. I'll even take you along to Fort Worth one of these times to buy some heads of cattle I plan to purchase once I buy more land. Would you like that, son?"

Billy bounced in his seat. "Yes, I would like to buy cattle. I'm really going to be a real cowboy, aren't I?"

Marshall grinned. "You sure are."

Ruby rode in silence. Their banter was sweet. How was she going to leave all of this behind? Once she had her land certificates back, where was she going to go? Should she stay in town with her aunt until she could decide where to go? Which reminder her, she needed to talk to Aunt Adeline.

Today.

The wagon stopped in front of the mercantile. "You two go on inside and pick out what you need. Billy, get yourself a good pair of boots. You're gonna need them come Monday."

"You leaving Monday?" Ruby asked.

Marshall looked at her. "Early in the morning on Monday. We'll take the cattle to Dallas, where they can load the cattle trains. It won't be a long drive, about two weeks."

Ruby chewed her bottom lip as she waited for Marshall to help her from the wagon. She remembered his puzzled look the last time and decided she'd try to behave. He took her hand as she stepped down from the bench. Looking in to his eyes, a spark flew between them. She closed her eyes, trying to shut it out of her mind.

He let go of her hand and turned away. As he walked away, he told her, "I'll see you in a bit."

Grabbing Billy by the hand, they went in to the mercantile. An older gentleman was behind the counter, wire-framed glasses and graying hair. "Ma'am," he said, nodding to her and the boy. "You must be the Mrs. Montgomery we are all hearing about. Welcome to Wichita Falls."

"Thank you, kindly, sir."

"Names Jim Wheeler. You can call me Jimmy. Everyone does."

"Nice to meet you, Jimmy."

"Is this the boy?" Jimmy nodded to Billy, who was leaning over a shelf staring at a wooden toy train.

She smiled and nodded. "Sure is. He needs a pair of boots."

Jimmy came around the counter to help Billy get fitted. The boy was reluctant to walk away from the wooden toy but did so when the older man held up a pair of pointy-toed boots. "I'll help him," Ruby called out, elated to finally get her land certificates back.

"Take off your shoes, boy. The lady will help you as I see I have another customer approaching."

Ruby was glad someone else came in to the store, distracting the owner. She didn't need an audience when she unveiled her property. A satisfied grin crossed her face.

The boy sat on the wobbly chair beside a pot-bellied stove in the middle of the store, his shoes off, feet dangling, not quite reaching the floor. Ruby snatched the shoes from his lap. She looked inside one shoe and then the other. Placing her hands inside, she wiggled her fingers around but there was nothing there.

When she looked at Billy and saw the satisfied smirk on his face, she wanted to scream. "Where are they?" she seethed, her voice low enough for him to hear but not loud enough for the mercantile owner or his customer.

"I hid them."

"What! You little conniver. Where? Right now, you tell me or I'm going to Marshall about this whole mess. Then you won't be able to stay at the ranch any longer."

He crossed his arms. "Neither will you. Then where will you go without them?"

"Billy, why are you doing this?" She knelt down, her face close to his. "I just want to get what belongs to me and leave."

He shrugged. "I know. I want to stay. I like it here."

"You can stay. It is your home now. I want to make my own way. Those land certificates are like gold to me. Please, Billy. Give them back."

"If I do, you will leave."

"Yes."

"I like you."

Ruby sighed. "Billy, I like you, too."

"I'll think about it."

Ruby tapped her toe against the wooden planks on the floor. She thrust a boot towards the boy. "Here, try this on." Where on earth would he hide them? Apparently, they were somewhere in his room. It was the only place he was before coming in to town.

She leaned forward, pretending to help him with his boots. "You've got one last chance, Billy. I guess it won't hurt for me to stick around while Marshall is on the cattle drive. That means you have two weeks to deliver the goods. Or else. Understand?"

"Two weeks?"

She nodded.

"Okay. I'll give them to you in two weeks."

"Swear to God."

His eyes went back and forth as if God were indeed watching him. Then he raised his little hand to his heart. "I give you my word."

"You sure? Cause if I don't get them back, you won't have a home either. We'll both be booted off the ranch."

His eyes widened. "I promised you I would. In two weeks. I don't want to go back to the city."

There was no sense in trying to reassure him. She raised her brows with a stern look. "Make sure you hand them to me by the time Marshall gets back."

"Gets back? What's that you say?" Marshall strode up to them, smiling.

Ruby stepped back, worried he heard them talking. "I, uh, told him that we would come back in to town when you get back. He loves it here so much."

Marshall's brow went up in that familiar way. He gazed at her a moment then shifted to Billy. "Here, son. Let me show you how a cowboy puts on a pair of boots."

While Marshall helped Billy with the boots, she had Jimmy gather up the things she needed, including one little wooden toy train.

Chapter 7

Marshall wanted to kiss her goodbye. After all, she was his wife. For the past few days, he stayed inside after their evening meal, helping her with cleaning up the kitchen. She had given in with a smile, letting him help after trying to shoo him away several times. He had been relentless, insisting on giving her a hand.

They fell in to a routine. The boy would come inside after spending much of his time with the hands and the three of them enjoyed each others company. Almost as if they were a real family. Their sleeping arrangements had worked so far. She usually fell asleep long before he would go to bed. Sometimes he'd sit on the rocker in the room, staring at the fire, dozing off like he used to, slipping out in the early morning hours before dawn.

"Would the two of you care for some apple pie?" she asked, smiling. Billy was sitting at the one end of the table, while Marshall read his paper alongside the boy. It was starting to feel too familiar. The boy would patiently sit by him while he read. Sometimes, he'd read aloud if he thought the boy would be interested in the article. Most times, Billy acted like he was but Marshall didn't doubt his mind was somewhere else. At least he seemed happy to be living on the ranch.

It was their last night together before heading out on the trail. He'd be gone for two weeks. Marshall planned to leave Max here, even though he needed him on the trail. Normally, he'd let one of the other ranch hands behind but trusted Max to protect them if need be. He wouldn't let the two alone, no matter how much he showed Billy about living on a ranch. They weren't ready yet. It was his job to protect his wife and the boy. He'd do whatever it took, even if he had to go off short-handed.

His wife disappeared for a moment. When she returned, she walked up to Billy. "I got something for you."

Billy looked up at her with fear in his eyes at first. Marshall wondered what that was all about? "For me?" the boy asked.

She brought her hand from around her back and placed a small, wooden train on the table in front of the boy. His eyes got so round, Marshall thought they would split open. His mouth opened but no words came out.

She turned and went back to her work.

Billy reached out and touched the train as if it were a fragile piece of glass. His hand slid over the wooden structure. Then he gathered it in both his hands. "May I be excused?" he asked, his voice husky.

Marshall nodded.

Billy rose out of the chair, took a few tiny steps in his new boots over to where she was working, her back to him.

He reached up and put his arms around her waist. "Thank you," he mumbled, his face in her skirt. Then the sound of booted heels flew across the room before hitting the steps to his room. A soft thump sounded as the bedroom door closed shut.

Marshall pushed himself away from the table. He moved over to where she stood with her back to him. No sound came from her but he could see her shoulders shaking. She tried hard to keep her emotions intact. Didn't she know he was here for her? If not, it was time she realized she didn't have to carry her burdens alone.

"Hey," he said, his voice low, sturdy and strong. "That was a nice thing you did for Billy." His hand rested on her shoulder.

She sniffed. He smiled. He pulled her against him. Her cheek rested on the back of his hand. They stood like that for a moment before she put her hands back in the dish water, pretending her act of kindness didn't happen.

Marshall sighed. He was going to miss her. "I'll be gone in the morning."

She turned to look at him, her eyes red and glassy. A tear tried to roll from her eye but he caught it with his finger and pushed it from her cheek.

Blue eyes stared at him. "How long will you be away?"

"I'd say a few weeks at the most. I'm leaving Max here to keep an eye on the ranch. Things will go on as usual, but you won't have as many mouths to feed."

His hand was still on her shoulder. It felt warm and nice. He leaned closer, taking in her scent that surprisingly smelled like lavender.

It almost seemed as if she were going to lean in to him. Then she took a deliberate step away and dried her hands. "I need some air," she said. "Care to sit on the back porch?"

Marshall smiled when she didn't wait for him but went through the door like her skirts were on fire. Was he affecting her? Rightly so, he grinned. At first he thought he wanted her in name only. After what they shared in the last few days, he realized he needed more than a wife in name only. He got the feeling she felt the same way. When he got back from the cattle drive, Marshall was going to tell her so.

Sitting on the back porch, enjoying the star-filled night was like heaven on earth with her. Long after they should be in bed, their rockers pressing in to the wooden boards, back and forth, the night air and silence of the dark night surrounding them, they enjoyed the company of each other. At one time, Marshall placed his hand over hers and she turned and smiled, her eyes hooded and barely open.

"Guess we should be off to bed," he said.

She nodded but didn't make a move to get up. Neither did he.

An hour later, she got up. He waited for her to go inside before trailing in after. He wanted to make sure she was tucked in and fast asleep before he entered the room. For him, it wouldn't do any good to try to sleep yet, not with her looking so beautiful tonight.

Marshall ran a hand through his hair. It was going to be a long, restless night on that rocking chair again.

<><>

Ruby stood in the yard waving. Marshall, the ranch hands and cook wagon were heading out to take the cattle to the rail road in Dallas. They'd be gone two weeks, he'd said. Seemed like a long time. Why did she care? Something was happening here to her she didn't understand. How did she develop feelings for this man? That was not supposed to happen.

"Oh, dear. I'm in deep trouble."

Max came across the yard with the wagon. "I'm going in to town. Anyone want to ride along?"

"Sure do. Let me get Billy." Ruby scampered around, finding Billy on the porch petting a stray cat. "We're going to town, hurry."

"The kitten needs some milk." He was scrunched down on his knees. Ruby got closer and sure enough, it was shaking and looking like it got lost from its mother. It appeared Billy had a soft spot for strays these days.

"Hold on, Max, don't leave without us," she told the foreman. He nodded and waved as she ran in to the house for some buttermilk. Scraping the cream off the top, she poured it in a small bowl and placed it on the porch. "We need to be off, Billy."

Reluctant to leave the kitten, Billy's steps were slow until he reached the wagon. "Will I be able to keep her?" he asked, jumping in to the back.

She shrugged. "I'm not sure it needs a home. It's mama may be looking for her right now."

"Really? I wish my mama was still here."

Shivers ran down her spine. She had been so intent on getting those land certificates, Ruby had forgotten he was a boy who lost his mother. Ashamed, she reached back and patted his arm. "My mama was dying when I left too, Billy. We're two peas in a pod with both of us losing someone we love."

"Why did you leave if she was dying?"

Oh, the questions of children. Ruby sighed. "She made me promise to go and bought me a ticket." Her brow shot in the air, reminding him he was the little thief who stole her ticket in the first place.

He squirmed in his seat, his eyes downcast. It made her realize Billy was changing. In front of her, day by day, he was becoming the ten year old boy he was meant to be, not some pan handler from the alleys of New York City. Marshall was right, this place was good for him. She'd miss him, too.

The reason Ruby wanted to go along to town was to see Aunt Adeline. She hadn't gotten a chance the last trip. Now that Marshall wasn't around to interfere, even if he didn't realize he would be, she'd be able to search the house for those land certificates. They had to be in the house somewhere, most likely in Billy's room. Talking to her aunt would help her decide upon her options for the future.

Except there seemed to be a problem arising. It seemed to Ruby her future was playing out right here in a nutshell. With Marshall. Raising Billy. She couldn't. No. It wasn't in her plans. She would be an independent woman no matter what. Determined, Ruby rode the rest of the way to town in silence.

<><>

The white clapboard house sat almost tight against another of the same type of house. A freshly painted sign on a makeshift post read *Adeline's Boarding House* in broad, white letters. Ruby followed Max up the steps and stood with him as he knocked on the porch. "Do you know Aunt Adeline?"

"Everyone knows your aunt," he laughed, his hearty tone loud. Someone called from the street as Max turned and waved.

When the door opened, Max pulled the cowboy hat from his head. He held it in front of him. There was a smile on his face a mile wide. "Miss Adeline," he said, his voice a bit softer.

"Good afternoon, Mr. Maximilian. Such a pleasure to see you," a strong, feminine voice sang out.

Ruby took it all in. She realized Max was sweet on her aunt, which made Ruby smile. Max was a decent man, too, like his boss. "Aunt Adeline, is that you?" she whispered, stepping around Max.

"Ruby?"

She nodded, tears forming in her eyes. She never met her mother's youngest sister but the instant their eyes met, it was as if they had known each other all along. Adeline held out her arms. "Come here, child," she crooned and took Ruby in to her arms and her home as if she was a long lost child welcomed home. Billy and Max followed the two in, standing in the doorway as they hugged each other.

When Ruby turned around she smiled at Billy, who had

taken his hat off as well, standing alongside of Max like a grown up. "Billy, meet my Aunt Adeline."

"It's Addy, you call me Addy, okay? Let's get you settled at my table and we'll talk over some tea. Would you like some tea, Billy?"

"No, ma'am. I'm going to go with Max to the mercantile. We need some supplies for the ranch."

Addy walked over to Max. "Is this true, Mr. Maximilian? You're leaving me so soon?" she crooned in her soft voice. When he agreed with the boy, she let them out the door and turned to Ruby with red cheeks.

It appeared that her aunt may be a bit soft on Max, too. Ruby looked around as her aunt made two cups of tea. "Your house is beautiful," she told her. Curtains hung on each window, darkening the room yet letting in enough light, giving the space a homey feel. "I should sew some curtains for the ranch," she mentioned, then realized what she just said.

"I'm so glad you came to visit. I heard you were here," Addy told her as she sat in the chair opposite Ruby. "I knew you were heading this way, your mama sent me a letter telling me so. When they said a Catherine Ruby was marrying our Marshall, I was pretty certain it was you. Just can't figure out where the Catherine came from."

Our Marshall? Oh, dear. It sounded like the whole town was in love with Marshall Montgomery. This may be harder to pull off after all. She wouldn't be able to buy a house and live in town if everyone knew and loved her husband. She'd be worse off living here. That meant she'd have to leave. Move on to another area. A chill went through Ruby.

"Well, now, tell me how your mama is?" Addy said, her soft voice filled with empathy.

"When I left, she wasn't doing too well. Perhaps by now she may be gone. I can't bear to think of her that way," Ruby spit out, her voice rising in grief and fear.

"Now, now. It's part of life, my dear. I'm sure that dratted brother of mine will post a letter to me. At least he won't get the land certificates. She did give you your inheritance, right?"

Ruby nodded. "I sort of have them."

"What? You will need them for the ranch. I must tell you that Marshall plans to extend his ranch. He wants to buy the property next to his except he doesn't have the money until the cattle drive is over. I just hope it isn't too late by the time he comes back. Heard a rumor some big rail road man is coming to town to buy up all the surrounding land, including what Marshall wants. Your certificates would come in handy if he isn't back by then."

Ruby grabbed her aunt's hand. "I don't plan to stay married to Marshall."

A slight twitch at the corner of her aunt's mouth was the only thing that led Ruby to believe Addy was surprised at the words she just spoke.

"Why not?"

Ruby wondered that herself. The ranch was so beautiful and she had a house over her head, plenty of food to eat and a ready made family with Billy and all. "It isn't in my plans, Aunt Addy. I want to be an independent woman. Like you."

Ruby watched her aunt struggle with her next words. "Sometimes, my dear, life rolls out another plan. You have to be prepared to take on whatever life dishes out. Why don't you know where your certificates are?"

Ruby told her about Billy stealing her purse. When she finished, her aunt had a smile spread from ear to ear. Then she laughed out loud. "I'm so sorry, dear. I'm not laughing at you but the boy is a corker. He's going to be just fine with Marshall and the ranch."

"Laugh all you want, Aunt Addie, but my certificates are somewhere hidden in the ranch house. As soon as I return home, I'm going to tear that house apart until I find them."

"Then, do what?" she asked, the blue eyes staring in to Ruby's soul. Her aunt had the same kind eyes like her mothers. It was eerily relieving in a way, kind of like her mother was here with her through someone else.

Ruby shrugged. "Not sure, but I want them back. They belong to me. I thought since everyone in town loves Marshall so much, I'll go somewhere else to buy land and build a home for myself."

Addy took her hand. Ruby stared at the table, their hands entwined, feeling as if her mama was right there. "Your mother was as stubborn as you, Ruby. When she came here and married your father, everyone hated her decision. Our parents shunned her. When your father died, she didn't know where to turn. She gave up everything to make sure you had a dry roof over your head. I told her she could stay here, but she was scared and alone. Years ago, this town was filled with railroad men, there was no law and it was hard for a woman to get by. Without her husband, she thought going back to New York was the right thing to do. Our brother treated her awful, made her dependent on him, even though she got him out of trouble many times with her own land certificates she sold. I vowed to never allow anyone to run my life."

Ruby nodded, clung on to her hand a little harder. "That's what I want, too. My uncle hated us, berated mama for having to come back home after being out here with scallywags and heathens."

"Is that what he said?" Addy laughed out loud.

"He did. Told Mama she'd have to cleanse her soul for the rest of her life. Mama got him out of his gambling debt many times over the years by selling those same certificates on occasion. But the last two, she gave them to me. Said she wanted more for me than to rely on anyone else."

Ruby heard her aunt sigh. "I understand. I felt the same way, Ruby. Let me tell you this. Sometimes in life we have to make a decision that is more important than anything we want. Sometimes it winds up being about someone else, a higher meaning."

Ruby rubbed a hand across her forehead. "I'm so confused."

"Do you like Marshall?" Addy asked, her gentle tone soothing to Ruby's ears.

She stared at her aunt. "I think so. I'm not sure what I feel, Aunt Addy. I know he is a kind man. But I have my mind made up to find a piece of land and build a home for myself, one no one can take from me."

Someone knocked on the door. Max and Billy returned from the mercantile. They both got up from the table to get the door. Before Addy let the others in, she turned to Ruby. "Perhaps the piece of land you seek is right there, in front of you all along."

Chapter 8

Ruby kept going over the words her wise aunt had said the other day when they went to town. She peeked out the window to watch Billy mucking out the stables with Max. Now was as good a time as any. She trudged up the wooden steps, turning the knob to the door to Billy's room.

The blanket was mused up on his bed. Even though she tried to teach him how to make his bed every morning, Ruby grinned at the boy's sad attempt. The wool blanket was crooked, hanging longer on one side. She went over to straighten it out when she realized he would know she was in here snooping.

Except she warned him she was going to find her property. *You would think by now the boy would just hand them over!* She searched in the dresser, pulling out the wooden drawers and placing a hand in between the shelves. Nothing. Ruby peeked under the mattress to find nothing but a few stray feathers from the mattress lying about. She reached out to gather up the strays when her hand hit a board that didn't fit just right. It wasn't smooth like the other ones. Using her knees and arms, she pushed the bed a few inches out of the way. Ruby got on her hands and knees to see close up. Sure enough, a piece of the wooden floor was loose.

Ruby nudge it with her hand until the chunk of wood revealed a small hole in the floor. She felt her way around the hole when it hit exactly what she was looking for. Smiling, Ruby extracted the land certificates from the hiding spot. She unfolded them to make sure they were hers. Satisfied, she quickly folded them back up, shoving them deep in the pocket of her dress.

Freedom at last! Ruby stood up on shaky knees, moved the bed back and strolled from the room, taking the steps carefully back down to the kitchen. She looked outside again to see Billy and Max taking a break. They sat on the fence, Billy's legs dangling alongside of Max, munching on an apple. "I got them, you little thief," she mouthed, knowing he would never notice her peeking from the window. A twinge of regret sang in her heart. She would miss him. Ruby didn't realize until that very moment she had developed a soft heart for the boy.

Yet he had taken from her at a time when she was most desperate. She had to stand strong, wasn't that what Addy would do? Perhaps it was time to take Marshall aside and reveal the truth to him, no matter the cost. He was a nice, caring man who wanted to make his life wholesome and worthwhile, to build a ranch and family. She couldn't stay here pretending to be someone else. That wouldn't be right. It wasn't fair to him. If a man fell in love with her, she wanted it to be true love between two people. Not loving someone he thought she was. Would he let her go on her own when he found out that she wasn't Catherine Jackson?

Ruby took a deep breath. Letting it out slowly, she picked up a basket for some apples. With her mind made up, she decided to stay until he returned and tell him the truth. Billy was secure here and Marshall would never turn him away, no matter that he stole from her. He had also found a soft spot in his heart for the boy, she knew this with all her heart and soul. She probably embellished to the boy how awful it was to steal. Perhaps it was why he didn't give them back all along, even after he was accepted here. That meant Ruby was just as responsible for letting this get long out of hand.

Perhaps it was time Ruby Adams made things right again.

Nothing ever seems to go as planned. That should be Ruby's motto, she thought with a sigh. Exactly one day before Marshall was due to return from the fourteen day cattle drive, Aunt Adeline came bursting on to the ranch property, frantic and yelling for the horses to slow down. It was the first time Ruby saw her aunt so excited.

She pulled the horses to a halt, unwound the reins from her arms, pulled up her skirts and jumped off the wagon like a woman on a mission. Ruby admired her zest and ran up to her. "What's wrong, Addie, is everything okay?"

"No, Ruby, it isn't. Where's Maximilian?" She let her skirts fall to the ground, turned and headed towards the barn when Addie pointed that way.

"Aunt Addie, what's wrong?" Ruby fell along side of her, her long legs trying hard to keep keep up with her aunt.

"It's all gone horribly wrong," she muttered, waving when Max came out of the barn.

When he noticed Addie, he began to high-step it towards her. "Miss Addie, what is it?"

"Byron Ward, that's what. He's here, in Wichita Falls."

Max spit, wiping the back of his hand over his mouth. "Excuse me, ma'am. This isn't good news. What did he say?"

"He has a meeting with some other big-time ranchers first thing in the morning, then he's going to the land office at noon to purchase all the land from here to hell evidently."

"Sonofabitch!" Max swore under his breath. He tipped his hat. "Excuse me again, ma'am. Mrs. Montgomery."

Ruby watched the exchange. "What is going on? Please, will someone tell me?"

For a moment, her aunt had looked so vulnerable, leaning towards Max. Like he would protect her. Then she watched as her aunt squared her shoulders. "Max, go after him.You and Billy ride like the dickens, he must be close enough he can get to town by noon tomorrow. I can stay right here with Ruby. I'll have a fresh horse ready and saddled. Go."

Max turned and motioned Billy to follow. Ruby watched in silence as the two saddled up and took off for God knows where.

"Lord, be with them. If this is your will, let the outcome be one we can all bear. Amen." Addie turned towards the house. "I sure could use a cup of tea."

Ruby followed her aunt to the kitchen, where she worked for some time in silence making tea as Addie wore a hole in the floor walking back and forth in the kitchen, her mind in deep thought. Ruby didn't want to disturb her mood, which seemed pretty dark at the moment.

She sat the two cups of tea down on the table. "Aunt Addie, come have some tea." The woman sat in the same seat Marshall always occupied. Ruby missed him.

Addie stirred the liquid after adding a bit of sugar from the small covered jug on the table. "It's starting to look like a woman's kitchen in here."

Ruby blushed. "I want to make curtains and a few other changes some day," she told her aunt, then stopped when realizing there would be no someday. Not if she left here.

Addie didn't miss a beat. "Ruby, when are you going to face facts. You don't want to leave here, do you?"

Her aunt was right. She had been struggling with her feelings all night. It had kept her up until early hours of the morning. Ruby finally got up from her bed to sit outside in the dark, on the porch where Marshall and her spent their last evening together, watching the stars fade from the night. "I don't want to leave." Those simple words made her cry. Deep, racking sobs that came out in such a fury Ruby didn't know what to do. She hung her head, letting the tears fall until Addie scooped her in her arms and held her until the tears fell away.

"It's all going to be alright, sweet Ruby. Now stop the tears. Independent women are not allowed to cry like this. It's time we talked."

"I'm sorry. I know I sound weak and all but," Ruby couldn't finish before more tears fell.

Addie gave her one last hug before sitting back down. "Now you listen to me, Ruby. I don't want you to be like me. I want you to be like you. A woman can still be independent and love a man with all her heart. It isn't like you think. What happened to your mama was unfortunate but you can't let your whole life be daunted by that one incident. Your uncle is an idiot and cruel to boot. You will always, always have me to fall back on if things don't work out here. You and Marshall are already married. Why don't you try to fall madly and deeply in love with him. It's a good thing you have going on right here. Don't run from what God has planned for you."

"I cheated, lied and I don't know if he will want me when I tell him the truth."

"How did you lie, Ruby? Tell me everything."

She did. Ruby told her how she met the woman at the train station and pretended to be Catherine Jackson, intending on paying the ticket back after she found the boy. "That's when I thought I would come clean and you know the rest. How Billy coerced me in to pretending I was someone else so he wouldn't get in to trouble. I followed along just like a puppy does."

Addie smiled. "I never did believe in coincidences my dear. I think perhaps there is a higher hand in all of this. Why don't we wait to see how it pans out."

"I'm going to tell him the truth the moment he returns."

"I wondered why you said your name was Catherine Ruby Jackson. Now, I know. Are you sure it is something you want to share with him? You are Ruby Montgomery, like it or not."

"I'm Catherine Ruby Montgomery. Not the same person, I'm afraid. Sad to say but we aren't truly married after all. He needs to know the truth. I'll take it from there. At least I'll have these land certificates if he throws me to the wolves." Another tear fell. Ruby brushed it away. She felt deep in her pockets and pulled the land certificates out. Opening them up, she spread the two on the table. "This is what I thought I wanted all along, Aunt Addie. Now, it feels empty thinking about living by myself on a piece of land without anyone to share it with. What happened to me?"

"I'd say Marshall Montgomery and a little boy name Billy happened." Her soft words spoke to Ruby's heart.

"You're right. Aunt Addie?"

Her aunt answered with a smile and the slight lift of her brow. "Yes, dear?"

"Can you drive me back to Wichita Falls? There's something more important than me that I have to do."

"Of course, dear."

"You were right. What I was seeking was right here all along."

<><>

"We'll head out at first light. Water the horses and make sure they are rested, ready to travel at heavy speeds," Marshall told two of his hands. They were on their way back from Dallas, the money he needed to buy the property tucked away in his saddlebags. When Billy and Max rode up hell bent for leather to tell them Byron Ward was in town, Marshall swore up one side of heaven and down the other side of hell.

He was so close. The land he yearned for was right at his fingertips. Marshall cursed the rail road man for showing up now. He sat by the fire they made, realizing the night came upon them too fast to ride the spent horses any further. They'd have to start out at the crack of dawn to get to Wichita Falls before noon.

Max grumbled. "That man has been a sore spot in your side ever since you left the rail road, Marshall. You can't let him buy that land out from under you."

Marshall shook his head. "He won't. I have the money now to purchase it. Knowing Ward, he'll be late anyway. Thinks he can come and go as he wishes." Marshall spoke the truth but still worried Ward would pull a fast one on him. Byron Ward may have wanted everyone to think he was meeting at the land office at noon, but the early morning meeting may be the actual time. Deceiving people was how he got ahead in the world.

Although, the land office didn't open until it felt like opening. Dawson, the owner, had a hard time with spirits and the fine ladies of the night. Ward wouldn't know where to find him. Marshall did.

"I have a confession to make," Billy said, his quiet voice surprising Marshall.

"Fess up, then."

"I stole something important." Billy hung his head.

Marshall knew there was something all along about the boy. He was glad his sister's child was going to be honest now. "What's that?" he said, his intent gaze on Billy's head.

The boy finally looked up to meet his eyes. Marshall thought he would grow up to be a fine cowboy. "When my mom and dad died, I didn't want to live with my grandmother. She yelled at me, telling me I should have died,too. I hated going home, hearing her tell me that every single day. I didn't want to go home after school, so I would hide in the ally behind the house. There were other kids there that showed me how to get things without money. It was stealing, I know now. I got in to trouble and my grandparents they said I had to come live with you."

Marshall put a hand on the boy's shoulder. "Son, no one should tell you those cruel words. I suppose they were having a hard time dealing with your mama's death. You have to forgive them so you can move on."

The boy nodded. "I don't want to go back to them, ever, Uncle Marshall. I'm sorry what I did to Ruby, I am."

Marshall began to worry. "What did you do?"

The little boy, who tried to be so grown up, wrung his hands together. He began to shake. "I'm afraid to tell you," he whispered.

"Why, Billy? Who scared you so?"

"Ruby did."

Marshall turned his head to look at Max but the older man shrugged. He scooted closer to the boy. "Billy, listen to me. No matter what you tell me, I will never, ever let you go back to your mean grandparents, I swear. You're my son now."

The boy's wide eyes stared up at him with all the trust in the world.

"Promise, right hand up to God?" he whispered, his voice filled with hope and a tad of trust.

"Right hand up to God," Marshall repeated.

The boy slumped in relief. "Good. I won't get hunged now?"

"You mean hanged? For what?"

"When we were on the train, Ruby told me that men got hung for stealing horses. What I did was worse."

That may have explained why there was so much tension between the two when he first met them. "Oh? What was it you did?"

"I stole her reticule when she was trying to board the train. It had her train ticket on and some important papers that I hid away."

Marshall didn't have to explain that stealing was bad. He had a hunch the boy already learned his lesson. When Billy went on to explain how some lady handed Ruby a train ticket, he began to realize she was indeed hiding something.

"The lady at the train station, she was the real Catherine

Jackson. I know, I saw her hand Ruby the letters. That lady was kissing a man, too. Right in front of everyone."

His letters? The ones he wrote to Catherine? Who was turning out not to be Ruby. A slow burn began deep in his gut.

"You mean to tell me Ruby isn't in fact one Catherine Jackson, that she was faking to be her so she could get a train ticket here?"

The boy nodded. "I didn't try to make her lie, too. It just happened. I was afraid you would send me back so I told her I would give her papers back to her when we got off the train. Then I made her come with us to your ranch. I didn't mean it, Uncle Marshall. I'm sorry. I just don't want Ruby to go any more."

"Why would she go, Billy?" Marshall was starting to put it all in perspective.

"She's gonna buy a house with land and give them papers to someone important. But I don't want her to go. Not any more."

"It's okay, Billy. We have a big job ahead of us. At first light, we're going to ride out of here to buy my own land. Think you can keep up?"

"I sure can!" Billy pulled a blanket off the saddle and rolled up in it near the warm fire. He was out in no time.

Marshall stared in to the fire long afterwards. "Seems my wife is not my wife," he told Max, who sat beside him, humming an old tune and carving a piece of wood with his knife.

"Seems so," Max mumbled. "Doubt that would make a difference to me. Beings you love her and all, I say it wouldn't matter."

"It does matter, Max. She lied to me."

"I think there's more to it than you realize. The boy took her belongings. Sounds like this was out of everyone's hands anyway."

Marshall grunted. "It doesn't matter. She lied, pretended to be my mail order bride. Why didn't she tell the truth when she got off that train?"

Max grinned. "Mayhap she liked what she saw."

"Shut-up, Max." Marshall was in no mood to kid around. He knew a stranger was coming in on that train but how could he let her raise a boy if she done nothing but lied since she got here. They had plenty of times to be honest. She seemed more worried about some papers Billy had than anything else.

In the morning, before he went to buy his land, he would tell her to pack her things and leave. He didn't need no lying woman by his side.

Chapter 9

The sound of horse's hooves pounded over the prairie. Ruby and Addie ran outside as the men came barreling in like a herd of cattle. "Get me a fresh horse," Marshall told Max, who went in to the barn first.

Ruby was about to tell him what she did when Marshall slid off his horse, anger all over his face. The corners of his mouth that she had wanted to kiss so badly turned down. The smile slid from her face.

The boy had already told him the truth. She could see it on his face. His eyes blazed with fury.

Ruby took a step back mortified. Marshall had been so kind. Now, he appeared so angry she wanted to shrivel up and hide in a hole somewhere. "I can explain," she said, her voice a bare whisper.

"No need." He was so close. She worried her bottom lip, pushed her hands deep in her apron as he grabbed her by the shoulders and kissed her in front of God and everyone. It wasn't a nice kiss at first, but one filled with anger and hurt. As quickly as it started, he began to kiss her softly, nibbling the bottom of her lip, stirring her insides like no one had ever done before. She raised her hands to his face, holding his cheeks in the palms of her hands as he pulled her closer and kissed her as if it were the last time he'd ever do it again. He forgave her. Didn't he? The more intense the kiss became, she knew.

It all became clear in that moment.

This was goodbye.

He pushed himself away. Stared in to her eyes for what seemed like forever. "Don't plan on being here when I return."

That was all he said before turning his back and walking away.

"I have to tell you something important," Ruby stammered, trying to find the right words.

Marshall put his booted foot in the stirrup and pulled himself to the saddle. "Save your lies for someone else," he told her before giving the horse a quick nudge. Before she could say another word, Marshall Montgomery was long gone.

Ruby wouldn't collapse like a log on the prairie. No, she was a strong, independent woman. Even if a tear rolled from her cheek. "I lost him."

A warm arm covered her shoulders. "Take it from me, Ruby. Don't ever say it's over."

"He looked at me with so much contempt I doubt I could ever make it up to Marshall." She choked on her words, covering her face with her hands. She didn't want Max and Billy to see her break down.

"Let's go inside," Addie ordered, taking her by the shoulders, helping her across the yard to the house.

"I'll get my things and say goodbye to Billy. I have to be gone before he comes back."

"I doubt he meant it, Ruby."

"He did, I know this to be true. At least one good thing has come of all this." Ruby smiled as she dabbed at a lone tear on her cheek.

"You gave it all up for him, Ruby. He'll come around. Don't leave. It would be a major mistake."

Ruby began to pack a few items in to her carpet bag she brought with her. It didn't take long to place what belonged to her inside. She unfolded the new land deed and placed it on the kitchen table, setting the sugar bowl on top.

"You can stay with me, Ruby."

"I have no where else to go now."

"I think you're wrong. Come to town with me. Spend a few nights here and then maybe when he's calmed down, he'll begin to see reason."

Ruby packed her lone piece of luggage into the back of Addie's wagon. She turned to Billy, who was frowning. "I didn't want you to go. Don't go, Ruby. I love you."

She ran to the little boy who had become a part of her life. Holding him in a big old hug, she lowered herself to his level. "You will always be a part of me now, Billy. I'll see you in town. I don't plan to be going anywhere soon. I love you, too."

Waving goodbye to Max, the two headed towards Wichita Falls. "I plan to earn my keep," she told her aunt.

"Pooey, girl. You're my relative. No need to."

"I'm not sure I can stay here knowing he is so close. If I can't, I may need to buy a ticket to go back home. The only way I can do that is to get a job. I have nothing left." She felt empty inside but it wasn't because of no money or land. It was because she had fallen head over heels in love with a man who despised her.

How would she ever make things right again?

Marshall knew he was pushing the horse to its limits. "Come on, you can do this," he urged. One more mile to Wichita Falls. He let the reins slacken a bit and checked his pocket watch, then slammed the cover shut with a click. Ten minutes to ten. Plenty of time according to his watch. Even so, he was desperate to get there before Ward pulled shenanigans.

His anger had dissipated since leaving the ranch. He wasn't even sure why he let it get the best of him. Seeing her standing in the ranch yard, waiting for him to come home had tugged at his own heartstrings. Billy was so happy to see her, too.

In that moment he had ached to pick her up and cover her in kisses. The reality hit him so hard he had made himself so angry. All he knew was he couldn't be with her knowing she had lied to him. Ruby with the sky blue eyes. It made his heart race thinking of her sitting on the porch with him, looking up at the stars, placing her hand in his every single night. Yet, it was all a lie, all pretense. He thought at first he could live without love. Then she started spending time with him each night, enjoying each others company. Just like a real marriage. It wasn't to be.Why hadn't he seen this? Had he closed his eyes to everything else?

Without realizing, Marshall nudged the horse even faster. She rode like the wind until the town came in to view. She galloped through the dirt street, straight to the land office. Marshall left her tied there, drinking up water from the metal trough. He had some land to purchase. Making his ranch bigger would take all his time and energy. Not a lot left to think about a woman with blue eyes. He turned from the land office and headed for the room Dawson usually spent the night at. Banging on the door, he turned the knob to find it wide open. The woman Dawson had dallied with was gone.

"Mornin' Dawson. Wake on up now, we have some business to tend to."

Dawson grumbled as usual. He was still in the bordelo on Main street, in a back room where the girls had a tiny broom closet of a room to sleep in, away from their daily lurid activities. Exactly where Marshall knew he would be. That meant one thing, Bryon Ward didn't stand a chance buying the land out from under him now. "I'm here to purchase a parcel or two of land."

"The land with the waterfall you've been harping about for the last two years?"

"That same land," Marshall told him. "Hurry, I need to get this transaction over and done with before noon."

"Too late," Dawson grumbled.

A cold fear hit Marshall in the gut. "What do you mean too late?"

"Someone came by and bought it yesterday."

"Impossible. Ward was in meetings yesterday."

"Not Ward. Two ladies came bursting through my door with these two land certificates and demanded to purchase the land. I even argues with them but they were insistent." A big old smile fell across Dawson's face as he slid on his pants. "Come with me to the office. I'll show you whose name the land is now in."

Dawson stumbled down the stairs, tucking a shirt into his britches. Out side in the warm air, he lifted his face to the sky. "Ah, wonderful weather." His arms went above his head in a stretch. "I love Wichita Falls. Fresh air, better than city air any day. It's a great day to be alive."

"That I'll agree with. Come on, now. Show me who owns this land. Do you think they may sell it?" Marshall was hopeful these two women were passing through and could be bought. Many others did the same thing, bought some land only to turn around and resell their parcel when they realized it would take years of hard work, something they weren't willing to do. Most went back east after realizing it was too rough out west in a semi-lawless country.

Dawson struggled to pull a set of keys from his pocket. As they walked down the street, a wagon went by, slowly pulling up to the boarding house. Marshall stared straight ahead. He knew it was Ruby, he felt her presence. It didn't matter. He was done. He almost turned around right before following Dawson inside.

Dawson lit up the small lantern on his desk, blowing out the long wooden match. He fussed around in the top desk drawer before pulling the black ledger out. Taking his good old time, Marshall's jaw began to tighten. "Would you hurry up, Dawson. What are you dallying for?"

Dawson looked at his friend and laughed out loud. "I love this stuff. You got a good woman, Montgomery."

Marshall didn't tell his friend what had conspired earlier between his wife and himself. He was sure Dawson would hear soon enough. "Give me the names of the women." Marshall's voice sounded threatening but the two knew each other for years. It didn't faze Dawson one bit.

"I can't keep you in suspense like this any longer. Here's the owner of six hundred forty acres of land, including a waterfall and watering hole, smack dab rubbing up against your own land." He handed the ledger to Marshall.

Almost afraid to know, Marshall tugged the book from his hand. His eyes scoured over the names until he came to the last name. "Dawson, is this a joke?"

"Afraid not. Here. A check for the other land certificate that was purchased in your name. Congratulations, you've got yourself land and some money to boot."

Marshall was floored. He stood there, a finger on his name, one he hadn't put in the ledger. "Is this legal?" he asked.

"Rightly so. Mrs. Montgomery turned these in, asking for the land to be put in her husbands name. The check, I'm afraid, had to be given to you direct." He shoved the paper at Marshall, who stuffed it in his pocket without a glance.

"She did this for me. Before I came back from Dallas."

"Sure did. You best go on home and give her some loving. Was a mighty fine thing to do, Marshall."

The two shook hands before Marshall left the office in a haze. He worked his way to the saloon, needing a stiff drink. When the barkeep held up a bottle, Marshall nodded but never touched it to his lips. He turned and left, his body steadfast and determined as he walked towards the boarding house. First, he stopped at the parish to speak to Daniel Conner. When he did make it back to the boarding house, his fist knocked three times on the door.

The door opened. She stood there, dried tears on her cheeks. He wanted to pick her up in his arms and carry her to the parish. So he did. Bending down, he scooped her in his arms, turned and began the long walk back to the church.

"What are you doing, Marshall?" a man asked, tipping his hat to the lady in Marshall's arms.

"I'm going to marry my wife, proper this time," he said, gazing at her.

"Marshall, do you mean this? You have forgiven me for lying to you, not telling you?"

"I do."

He stopped outside the door of the parish, placing her on her feet. Taking her hands, he knelt down on one knee. "Mrs. Montgomery, will you forgive me for casting you off and marry me? This time as Ruby Adams, not Catherine Jackson?"

"Are we allowed to do this?"

"Daniel says so. He had been so busy he never filed our marriage certificate yet. Seems lady luck is with us. That means we can tear up that last certificate and start new. I'm so sorry, Ruby. I realized how much you cared when you gave up your own land certificates for me."

She placed her hands on his cheeks, bending down to kiss him squarely on the mouth. "Mr. Montgomery, I will marry you on one condition."

Marshall tensed. It was never a good idea to put conditions on things. He stared in to those perfect blue eyes knowing he would do anything she asked. "What is it, Ruby?"

She helped pull him up from his bent knee.They stood on the front porch, cheek to cheek as she whispered in his ear. "That you love me until the end of time, Mr. Montgomery."

A deep sigh escaped him. "That's easy, Ruby. I do love you. In these short weeks, I thought I would be getting a woman who would care for the farm and my nephew. Now, I have a woman I can't be away from longer than five minutes."

She tipped her chin in the air. "As I love you, Marshall Montgomery. I'd be proud to be your wife. Again. This time the marriage will be consumated. Tonight." She stole a quick kiss and marched into the parish, like a woman on a mission.

Marshall followed like a lost puppy who finally found his way home. He patted his pocket with the folded up check. Now he didn't have to go out on another cattle drive so soon. Winter was approaching. They could spend the cooler nights together, curled under the blankets or by the fire, as man and wife. Even though Texas didn't get as cold as some places, the nights would be perfect for what he had in mind.

"Are you coming, Mr. Montgomery?"

"Yes, Mrs. Montgomery. Let's get married, again."

He let the door of the parish slam as he hurried to conclude the ceremony that would make her his true wife.

Perhaps Dawson was right. It was a great day to be alive.

****Thanks for reading Ruby. Turn the page to find about a reader exclusive for free.****

Reader Exclusive

This book will not be published to Amazon. It is a backstory of how Miss Addie came to Wichita Falls and the man she actually fell in love with before putting her heart and soul into the pioneer town of Wichita Falls. Go get yourself a copy!

Miss Addie: The Beginning. Get your free copy here!
(http://www.cyndiraye.com/miss-addies-story/)

****

For a current list of all the books for the Brides of Wichita Falls series, go to my Author Amazon Page.
(https://www.amazon.com/Brides-of-Wichita-Falls/e/B06XCR9L7J)

Made in the USA
Las Vegas, NV
27 August 2022